The Mechanism of Memory

A hidden device. A buried truth.

A past waiting to be unlocked.

MARIA KARRA

Published by FRESNEL PRESS
12781 Orange Grove Blvd
West Palm Beach, FL 33411
United States of America

Printed in the United States of America

ISBN: 978-1-958312-37-7

For A.J.H., who keeps my life in motion,

even when the gears jam.

The Mechanism of Memory

CHAPTER 1

Astoria had a way of waking up slowly, as if the neighborhood stretched its limbs before deciding what kind of day it wanted it to be. On most mornings, Daphne Stavrides liked to sit by her window with a cup of coffee and watch the street come alive. Delivery trucks rumbled past the bakery on the corner, the scent of warm sesame bread drifting upward. Elderly men gathered outside the café, speaking in Greek with the kind of musical cadence she had always loved but never understood. The elevated train screeched overhead, rattling the windows in a way she found oddly comforting.

She had lived in this apartment for nearly a decade, long enough to memorize the rhythm of the neighborhood but not long enough to feel like she belonged to the Greek-speaking world that surrounded her. She was Greek-American, yes, but the Greek part had always felt like a distant inheritance — something she admired from afar but never fully claimed.

Her grandfather, Yiannis, had tried. He had always encouraged her to learn the language. He would slip

Greek words into conversations, smiling patiently as she repeated them with clumsy pronunciation. He would tell her stories about his childhood, pausing to translate the parts she didn't understand. He would bring her children's books in Greek, hoping she might pick up the alphabet the way children absorb things without trying.

But life had a way of filling itself with obligations. School, work, friends, deadlines — everything seemed more urgent than learning a language she heard only during holiday dinners or brief visits to her grandfather's house. And because he lived a few blocks away rather than under the same roof, she didn't hear Greek daily. Her parents spoke only English at home. Her cousins were the same. Greek was something she always meant to learn "soon," but soon kept drifting further away. Now, as she sat by her window sipping her coffee, she wished she had listened to him more closely.

Her phone buzzed on the table beside her. She glanced at the screen and saw her mother's name. It was early — too early for a casual call. A knot formed in her stomach.

"Hi, Mom," she answered, trying to sound calm.

Her mother's voice was soft, almost fragile. "Daphne… it's Papou. He passed away last night."

The world seemed to tilt. Daphne gripped the edge of the table, her breath catching in her throat. She had known this moment would come eventually — her grandfather was ninety-three, after all — but knowing something is inevitable doesn't make it easier when it arrives.

"When?" she whispered.

"Just after midnight. In his sleep. It was peaceful."

Daphne closed her eyes. She pictured her grandfather sitting in his favorite armchair, the one with the worn armrests and the crocheted blanket draped over the back. She pictured him smiling at her, offering her a plate of *koulourakia*, telling her stories about Lefkada, the island where he had grown up. She pictured him saying, as he always did, "One day, you'll go there. You'll see where our family began."

She had always nodded, promising she would. But she had never gone.

"I'll come over," she said.

The next few days passed in a blur of condolences, casseroles, and memories. The funeral was held at the Greek Orthodox church her grandfather had attended for decades. The incense, the chanting, the flickering candles — everything felt heavy with meaning. Daphne stood beside her mother, accepting hugs from relatives she barely knew, listening to stories about her grandfather's kindness, his stubbornness, his humor.

After the burial, the family gathered at her uncle's house. The living room was filled with the sound of clinking plates and murmured conversations. Daphne sat quietly on the couch, feeling both surrounded and alone. She kept thinking about the last time she had seen her grandfather. He had been sitting in his armchair, telling her about a book he was reading. He had asked her, as he always did, "Have you started learning Greek yet?"

She had laughed and said, "Soon, Papou. I promise."

Now the promise felt like a stone lodged in her chest.

Two days later, Daphne received a call from her grandfather's lawyer, asking her to come to his office for the reading of the will. She arrived early, sitting in the small waiting room with her hands folded in her lap. The walls were lined with framed certificates and photos of the lawyer shaking hands with various community leaders. A faint smell of old paper lingered in the air.

When her mother and uncle arrived, the three of them were ushered into a narrow office with a large wooden desk. The lawyer, a thin man with silver hair and wire-rimmed glasses, greeted them with a solemn nod.

"Thank you for coming," he said. "Mr. Papadakis left clear instructions regarding his estate."

He began reading the will, his voice steady and formal. Small sums of money were left to various relatives. A few heirlooms were distributed. Her uncle received the fishing rods her grandfather had cherished. Her mother received a set of hand-carved icons.

Then the lawyer paused and looked directly at Daphne.

"To my granddaughter, Daphne," he read, "I leave a sealed letter. She is to read it privately and must not show it to anyone."

Daphne blinked. "A letter?"

The lawyer nodded and reached into a drawer. He pulled out a thick envelope, yellowed at the edges, and handed it to her. Her name was written on the front in her grandfather's familiar handwriting — looping, elegant, unmistakable.

Her mother leaned forward. "What does it say?"

"I… I'll read it when I get home," Daphne said, slipping the envelope into her bag before her mother could reach for it.

The lawyer cleared his throat. "Your father was very specific. The letter is for Daphne's eyes only."

Her uncle raised an eyebrow. "My father was full of surprises."

Daphne didn't respond. Her heart was pounding. She felt the weight of the envelope against her side, heavier than paper should be.

When the meeting ended, she walked home alone, the envelope tucked safely in her purse. The streets of Astoria felt different somehow — sharper, louder, more vivid. She passed the bakery where her grandfather used to buy bread, the café where he played backgammon with his friends, the small grocery store where he insisted on choosing his own olives because "no one else knows how to pick them properly."

Every corner held a memory.

When she reached her apartment, she locked the door, sat at her kitchen table, and placed the envelope in front of her. She stared at it for a long moment, her fingers trembling slightly.

Finally, she opened it.

Inside was a single sheet of paper, filled with her grandfather's handwriting.

In Greek.

Daphne's breath caught. She recognized the alphabet — she had seen it on signs, in books, in the children's stories her grandfather had given her — but she couldn't read it. Not really. A few words looked familiar, but the rest was a maze of symbols she couldn't decipher. She tried sounding out the first line, stumbling over the letters. She recognized "αγάπη," love, and "σπίτι," house, but the rest was beyond her.

At the bottom of the back page were two small sketches: one showed Lefkada with "Nydri" marked on the east side and a dot nearby; the other resembled a floorplan with a staircase and a dot at its base.

She pulled out her phone and opened a translation app. She took a picture of the letter and waited as the app processed the text. The result was a jumble of nonsense about "the wind of the old house" and "the path of the hidden sun." She tried another app. It was worse. She considered searching for another app but felt as though she was betraying her grandfather. Although he had left her a message she couldn't decipher, she was confident it wasn't his intention for her to seek out easy solutions.

She pressed her palms to her forehead, frustration rising in her chest. She wished she had learned Greek when he encouraged her. She wished she had taken classes, practiced with him, listened more closely. She wished she had done a hundred things differently. But wishing wouldn't help her now.

She needed to learn Greek. Not someday. Not eventually. Now.

She stopped abruptly. Was this a trick? Was this her grandfather's way of making her learn Greek at last? Was that all there was to the letter? Perhaps the treasure was the Greek language itself. There was only one way to find out, and that was to read the letter.

"All right, Papou. You win," she said out loud, half-smiling.

She opened her laptop and typed "Greek tutor online" into the search bar. Dozens of results appeared, but one profile caught her eye.

Tasos Nikolaidis — Native Greek speaker, experienced tutor, patient and friendly.

His photo showed a man in his early thirties with warm brown eyes and a gentle smile. Something about his expression made her pause. He looked kind. He looked like someone who would understand if she stumbled, someone who wouldn't judge her for starting so late.

She clicked "Book a Trial Lesson."

As she closed her laptop, she felt a strange mixture of determination and fear. She didn't know what her grandfather had written. She didn't know why he had left her a private letter. She didn't know what secrets it held. But she was going to find out. Whatever it took.

CHAPTER 2

Daphne didn't sleep much that night. She lay awake staring at the ceiling, the letter resting on her nightstand. Every time she closed her eyes, she saw her grandfather's handwriting, the looping letters she had traced as a child when he taught her how to write her name in Greek. She remembered how proud he had been when she managed to form the letters correctly, how he had kissed her forehead and said, "You have the hands of a writer, *koukla mou.*"

She had always loved words. She had built a career around them. But now she was confronted with a message she couldn't read, written by the person she had loved most in the world. The irony stung.

When morning finally arrived, she made coffee and sat at her kitchen table with the letter in front of her. The sunlight illuminated the ink, making the words look almost alive. She tried again to decipher them, sounding out syllables, guessing meanings, hoping something would click. But the sentences remained stubbornly opaque.

She opened her laptop and searched for Greek alphabet charts, pronunciation guides, beginner lessons. She spent an hour trying to memorize the letters, whispering them under her breath. Alpha, beta, gamma, delta. She felt like a child again, except this time there was no grandfather sitting beside her, gently correcting her mistakes.

Her phone buzzed with a message from her cousin, asking how she was holding up. She typed a brief reply, then set the phone aside. She didn't want to talk about her grief. She didn't want to talk about anything except the letter, and she couldn't talk about that with anyone.

She returned to the tutoring platform and checked her upcoming lesson with Tasos. It was still two days away. She considered messaging him again, asking if he had time sooner, but she didn't want to seem impatient. She wanted to appear composed, even though she felt anything but.

She spent the rest of the morning working on a manuscript about a woman who moved to a small town to open a flower shop. The story was sweet, but Daphne found herself drifting in and out of focus. She kept glancing at the letter, as if it might reveal its secrets if she stared long enough.

By noon, she gave up on work entirely and decided to take a walk. The air outside was crisp, carrying the scent of roasted chestnuts from a street vendor. She walked past the café where her grandfather used to sit with his friends, their voices rising and falling in animated conversation.

She paused for a moment, listening to the familiar cadence of Greek. It felt like a language she had always been adjacent to but never fully embraced.

She continued down the street, passing the small grocery store where her grandfather had insisted on choosing his own produce. She remembered standing beside him as he inspected tomatoes, rejecting any that didn't meet his standards. "A good tomato smells like the sun," he used to say, lifting one to her nose so she could inhale its scent.

She smiled at the memory, then felt a pang of regret. She wished she had spent more time with him. She wished she had asked more questions, listened more closely, learned more about his life. She wished she had learned Greek when he encouraged her, instead of postponing it year after year.

She walked for nearly an hour before returning home. The letter was still on the table, waiting. She sat down and looked at it again, even though she knew she wouldn't understand it. She traced the words with her fingertip, imagining her grandfather writing them. She wondered what he had been thinking, what he had wanted her to know, why he had chosen to write in Greek instead of English.

She wondered why he had insisted she read it alone.

The thought sent a shiver through her. Her grandfather had never been secretive. He had been open, affectionate, generous. If he had written something he didn't want anyone else to see, it had to be important.

She folded the letter carefully and placed it back in the envelope. She needed to learn Greek. She needed to understand every word. She needed to honor his final request.

The next day passed slowly. Daphne tried to distract herself with work, errands, and cleaning, but her mind kept drifting back to the letter. She found herself counting down the hours until her lesson with Tasos. She felt a strange mixture of nerves and anticipation. She had never taken online language lessons before. She didn't know what to expect.

When the time finally arrived, she sat at her desk, adjusted her webcam, and took a deep breath. The call rang, and she clicked "Accept."

Tasos appeared on her screen, smiling warmly. His room was bright, with a bookshelf behind him filled with colorful spines. A small plant sat on the windowsill, its leaves catching the sunlight. He looked relaxed, friendly, approachable.

"Hello, Daphne," he said. "It's nice to meet you."

"Hi," she replied, returning the smile. "Nice to meet you too."

He asked her about her background, her connection to Greece, her goals for learning the language. She told him she was Greek-American, that her grandfather had always encouraged her to learn Greek, that she had always meant to start but never found the time.

Tasos nodded thoughtfully. "It's never too late to learn," he said. "And you already have a connection to the language. That helps more than you think."

He began with the basics — the alphabet, simple greetings, common phrases. Daphne stumbled through the sounds, tripping over the unfamiliar letters. Tasos corrected her gently, offering encouragement with every attempt. He had a calm, patient demeanor that made her feel at ease.

By the end of the lesson, she felt a small spark of confidence. She knew it would take her a while to become fluent, but she had taken the first step.

"Would you like to schedule another lesson?" Tasos asked.

"Yes," she said without hesitation. "Definitely."

They set a weekly schedule, and Daphne ended the call feeling lighter than she had in days. She closed her laptop and leaned back in her chair, letting out a long breath. She felt hopeful. She felt determined. She felt connected to something larger than herself.

Over the next few weeks, her lessons with Tasos became the highlight of her routine. She practiced diligently, repeating vocabulary words under her breath as she cooked, cleaned, or walked through the neighborhood.

She filled a notebook with Greek phrases, writing each one carefully, as if the act of writing could bring her closer to her grandfather.

Tasos proved to be an excellent teacher. He was patient, encouraging, and unexpectedly funny. He told stories about growing up in Athens, about his grandmother's cooking, about the quirks of Greek grammar. He had a way of making the language feel alive, vibrant, full of personality.

Daphne found herself looking forward to their lessons not just because she wanted to learn Greek, but because she enjoyed talking to him. She liked the way he smiled when she got something right, the way he tilted his head when he explained something complicated, the way his voice softened when he spoke about his family. He had a very strong accent in English, which Daphne found endearing. It reminded her of the Greek owner of her favorite Astoria pastry shop, who never lost his accent after decades in America. Growing up around Greeks in Astoria, including her grandparents, Daphne was used to English spoken this way and had no trouble understanding Tasos, even when he mispronounced words. She realized that she liked a lot of things about him, but she tried not to read too much into it. She reminded herself that he was her tutor, nothing more. But sometimes, when he looked at her with those warm brown eyes, she felt a flutter in her chest that had nothing to do with language learning.

He spoke English with a strong accent, which Daphne found endearing. She considered him a sweet man.

One afternoon, after a particularly good lesson, Daphne decided to try reading the letter again. She sat at her kitchen table, the envelope open in front of her, and scanned the lines slowly. This time, she recognized a few more words. "Ταξίδι." Journey. "Νησί." Island. "Λευκάδα." Lefkada.

Her heart quickened. She whispered the name aloud, tasting the unfamiliar syllables. Her grandfather had spoken to her many times about Lefkada, his homeland, but she had never imagined she might have a reason to visit besides tourism.

She leaned closer to the letter, squinting at a line near the bottom. She recognized the word "Θησαυρός." Treasure.

She sat back, stunned. Her grandfather wanted her to go to Lefkada. And he wanted her to find something valuable.

She felt a rush of excitement, fear, and curiosity all at once. She didn't know what the treasure was. She didn't know why he had hidden it. She didn't know why he had chosen her. But she knew one thing: she had to go.

She folded the letter carefully and placed it back in the envelope. She would continue her lessons. She would learn as much Greek as she could. And when she was ready, she would travel to Lefkada. She didn't know what she would find there. But she felt, deep in her bones, that

her grandfather had left her something important —
something meant only for her. And she was determined to
uncover it.

The weeks following her grandfather's funeral unfolded
with a strange mixture of heaviness and momentum.
Daphne felt as if she were living in two parallel worlds:
one where she moved through her daily routines with
practiced familiarity, and another where she hovered on
the edge of something unknown, something her
grandfather had set in motion long before she realized it.

Her mornings still began with coffee by the window,
watching Astoria wake up. The bakery still filled the air
with the scent of warm bread. The elderly men still
gathered outside the café, their voices rising in animated
Greek. But now, instead of feeling like an outsider
listening to a language she admired from afar, Daphne felt
a tug of recognition. She could pick out a few words here
and there — greetings, simple phrases, bits of vocabulary
Tasos had taught her. It wasn't much, but it was enough
to make her feel as if she were slowly stepping into a world
she had always been adjacent to but never fully entered.

Her lessons with Tasos had become a steady anchor in her
week. She practiced diligently, filling pages of her
notebook with Greek letters, vocabulary lists, and short
sentences. She repeated phrases aloud as she cooked
dinner, whispered conjugations while waiting for the
subway, and scribbled notes on sticky pads she stuck to
her refrigerator. She felt a quiet pride each time she

recognized a word in the wild, like spotting a familiar face in a crowd.

But beneath the progress and the routine, the letter remained a constant presence — a silent weight in her drawer, a reminder of the mystery she had yet to unravel. She read it every few days, hoping that her growing knowledge would unlock new meanings. Each time, she recognized a few more words, but the full message remained out of reach. It was like trying to assemble a puzzle with half the pieces missing.

One afternoon, after finishing a round of edits for work, Daphne decided to take the letter to her favorite café. She needed a change of scenery, a place where she could think without the distractions of her apartment. She tucked the envelope into her bag, grabbed her notebook, and headed out.

The café was a small, cozy spot tucked between a florist and a bookstore. It had mismatched chairs, exposed brick walls, and a chalkboard menu that changed daily. Daphne ordered a cappuccino and found a seat by the window. She spread out her notebook, opened the envelope, and placed the letter gently on the table.

She read the first line slowly, sounding out each word. She recognized "αγάπη" – love, "μακριά" – far, and "χρόνος" – year or time. She wrote them in her notebook, then moved to the next line. She recognized "σπίτι" – house and "παλιό" – old. She copied them, feeling a small thrill of accomplishment.

But the rest remained a blur.

She sighed and leaned back in her chair. She wished she could ask her grandfather what he meant. She wished she could sit with him one more time, listening to his stories, hearing his voice. She wished she had learned Greek sooner, when he was still alive to guide her.

A soft voice interrupted her thoughts.

"Studying?"

Daphne looked up to see a woman in her sixties standing beside her table. She wore a floral scarf and carried a canvas tote bag filled with books. Her eyes were warm, curious.

"Yes," Daphne said, smiling politely. "I'm learning Greek."

The woman's face lit up. "Ellinika? Very good! It's a beautiful language."

"I'm trying," Daphne said. "It's harder than I expected."

The woman laughed softly. "I know. Greek is very hard. But you'll get there. Just keep practicing."

She moved on, leaving Daphne with a small burst of encouragement. She returned to the letter, tracing the lines with her fingertip. She turned it over and traced the sketch of Lefkada. She spent another hour working through the letter, writing down every word she recognized, guessing at meanings, trying to piece together the fragments. When she finally packed up her things, she felt both frustrated and determined. She wasn't making progress fast enough. She needed more lessons. She needed more time. She needed to understand what her grandfather had left for her.

As she walked home, she passed the Greek grocery store her grandfather had loved. The owner, Mr. Stavros, stood behind the counter, arranging jars of olives. He looked up and waved.

"Daphne! Come in, come in."

She stepped inside, greeted by the familiar scent of herbs and brine. The shelves were lined with imported goods — olive oil, honey, spices, cheeses. Her grandfather had brought her here often when she was a child, teaching her the names of foods she couldn't pronounce.

"How are you, *koukla*?" Mr. Stavros asked, his voice gentle.

"I'm okay," she said. "Taking things day by day."

He nodded knowingly. "Your grandfather was a good man. Very proud of you."

The words hit her unexpectedly. She felt her throat tighten. "Thank you."

He reached under the counter and pulled out a small jar of honey. "This is from Lefkada," he said. "Your grandfather loved it. Take it."

She hesitated. "I can't—"

"It's a gift," he insisted.

She accepted the jar, feeling a warmth spread through her chest. She thanked him and left the store, holding the honey carefully in her hands. It felt like another thread connecting her to her grandfather, another reminder of the place he had come from.

When she reached her apartment, she placed the jar on her kitchen counter and stared at it for a long moment. She imagined the island where it had been made — the hills, the sea, the wildflowers.

She felt a pull toward that place, a pull she couldn't ignore.

That evening, during her lesson with Tasos, she found herself more focused than usual. She asked questions, took notes, repeated phrases with determination. Tasos noticed.

"You're very motivated today," he said, smiling.

"I want to make progress," she replied. "I have a lot to learn."

"You're doing well," he said. "Greek takes time, but you're picking it up quickly."

She hesitated, then asked, "Have you ever been to Lefkada?"

Tasos nodded. "Yes, a few times. It's beautiful. Very peaceful. The beaches are incredible."

She felt her heart quicken. "What's it like?"

He leaned back in his chair, thinking. "It's the kind of place where time slows down. The water is clear, the cliffs are white, and the villages feel untouched by the rush of modern life. People there are warm, welcoming. It's a place that stays with you."

Daphne felt a shiver run through her. She wanted to see it. She wanted to walk the same paths her grandfather had walked, breathe the same air, feel the same sun.

She wanted to understand the letter.

After the lesson ended, she sat at her desk, staring at the envelope. She knew she couldn't wait forever. She needed to go to Greece. She needed to follow the clues her grandfather had left. She needed to find whatever he wanted her to find. But she also knew she wasn't ready yet. She needed more language skills, more confidence, more clarity. She needed to prepare.

She opened her notebook and wrote a single word at the top of a fresh page:

Lefkada.

The word looked bold, decisive, almost unreal. She traced it with her fingertip, feeling a surge of determination.

She didn't know when she would go. She didn't know what she would find. But she knew she would make the journey.

For the first time since her grandfather's death, she felt a sense of direction — a path unfolding before her, leading her toward something meaningful, something she was meant to discover.

She closed her notebook, placed the letter gently inside it, and turned off the light. Tomorrow, she would move closer to the truth her grandfather had left behind.

CHAPTER 3

The next morning, Daphne woke with a sense of restless energy. She had dreamt of Lefkada — or at least, the version of it she had pieced together from photographs and her grandfather's stories. In her dream, the island shimmered with sunlight, the sea shifting between shades of turquoise and sapphire. She had walked along a narrow path lined with olive trees, the leaves whispering in the breeze, and she had felt her grandfather's presence beside her, warm and steady.

When she opened her eyes, the dream dissolved, but the feeling lingered.

She made coffee and sat by the window, watching the neighborhood stir to life. A delivery truck idled by the curb. A woman walked her dog, bundled in a coat despite the mild weather. A group of teenagers laughed as they passed the bakery.

Daphne sipped her coffee and opened her notebook. She flipped to the page where she had written "Lefkada". She felt a quiet thrill as she repeated it a few times out loud.

She wasn't ready to go there yet, but she was moving in the right direction.

She spent the morning reviewing vocabulary, practicing pronunciation, and writing simple sentences in Greek. She felt a small burst of pride each time she recognized a word from the letter. She still couldn't understand the full message, but the fragments were beginning to take shape, like pieces of a mosaic slowly falling into place.

Around noon, she received a text from her mother.

Dinner tonight? Your uncle is coming. We can talk about Papou.

Daphne hesitated. She loved her family, but she wasn't ready to discuss her grandfather's letter. She didn't want to lie, but she also couldn't break his instructions. She typed a reply.

I'll be there.

She spent the afternoon working, though her mind kept drifting. She edited a chapter about a character who discovered a hidden journal in her grandmother's attic. The parallels weren't lost on her. She wondered if the author had ever received a mysterious letter from a relative. She wondered if anyone else had felt the strange mixture of grief and anticipation she felt now.

When evening arrived, she walked to her mother's house, a brownstone a few blocks away. The door was open, and the smell of roasted chicken drifted into the hallway. Her mother greeted her with a tight hug, her eyes soft with lingering sadness.

"Hi, sweetheart," she said. "Come in."

Her father and her uncle were already seated at the dining table, sipping wine. Her father stood when he saw her.

"Daphne," he said warmly. "Come here, my girl. How are you holding up?"

"I'm okay," she said. "Taking things one day at a time."

They sat down to dinner, the conversation drifting between memories of her grandfather and updates on family members. Her mother talked about the church service, her uncle shared a story about fishing with Papou, and Daphne listened, feeling both comforted and distant.

At one point, her mother turned to her. "Did you read the letter? What did it say?"

Daphne felt her pulse quicken. She kept her expression neutral.

Her father jumped in: "Darling, you know that letter is personal."

Her mother nodded, though her eyes lingered on Daphne for a moment longer than necessary. Her uncle raised an eyebrow but didn't say anything.

Daphne felt a wave of relief. She didn't want to lie, but she also couldn't reveal the truth. At least not yet.

After dinner, she helped her mother wash the dishes. The kitchen was warm, the air filled with the scent of lemon soap. Her mother dried a plate and glanced at her.

"You know," she said softly, "your grandfather loved you very much."

"I know," Daphne said, her throat tightening.

"He always talked about how proud he was of you. He wished he could have spent more time with you."

Daphne swallowed hard. "I wish that too."

Her mother placed a hand on her shoulder. "Whatever he wrote in that letter, I'm sure it was important to him. Take your time with it."

Daphne nodded, grateful for the understanding. She hugged her mother goodbye and walked home under the glow of streetlights.

When she reached her apartment, she sat at her desk and opened the letter again. She read it slowly, her eyes tracing the familiar loops of her grandfather's handwriting. She recognized more words now — enough to sense the shape of the message, though not enough to grasp its full meaning. She saw references to Lefkada, to a house, to a journey, to something hidden. She saw the word "παλιό," old, repeated twice. She saw "θυμήσου," remember. She saw "θα βρεις," you will find.

She felt a shiver run through her. Her grandfather wanted her to find something. Something connected to his past. Something he had left behind.

She closed the letter and leaned back in her chair. She felt a mixture of excitement and fear. She didn't know what she would find in Lefkada. She didn't know what secrets her grandfather had kept. But she felt drawn to the island, as if it were calling her.

The next day, during her lesson with Tasos, she found herself distracted. She stumbled over simple phrases, mispronounced words she had mastered weeks ago, and lost her place in her notes.

"Are you okay?" Tasos asked gently.

"Yes," she said, forcing a smile. "Just a lot on my mind."

He nodded. "Learning a language can be overwhelming. It's normal to have days like this."

She appreciated his understanding, but she knew her distraction had nothing to do with grammar. She wanted to ask him more about Lefkada, about the culture, about the people. She wanted to ask him if he believed in fate, in family secrets, in the idea that the past could reach across time to guide the present.

Instead, she tried to focus on the lesson, determined to make progress. She repeated vocabulary words, practiced verb conjugations, and wrote short sentences in her notebook. By the end of the hour, she felt more grounded.

"Good work today," Tasos said. "You're improving."

"Thank you," she said. "I'm trying."

After the call ended, she sat at her desk, staring at the letter. She felt a growing urgency. She needed to know what her grandfather wanted her to do. She opened her laptop and searched for flights to Greece. She didn't book anything yet, but she looked at dates, prices, and routes. She imagined herself walking through the airport, boarding a plane, stepping onto Greek soil for the first time. She imagined standing on the shores of Lefkada, the sea stretching out before her, the cliffs rising behind her. She imagined finding the house her grandfather had written about, touching its walls, feeling the weight of history in the air. She imagined discovering the treasure he had hidden — whatever it was.

Over the next week, she threw herself into her studies. She practiced daily, reviewed old lessons, and asked Tasos for extra exercises. She felt a growing sense of purpose, a determination that surprised even her. She had always been diligent, but this was different. This was personal.

One evening, she decided to visit her grandfather's house. Her uncle had the keys, but he had told her she was welcome to stop by anytime. The house was only a few blocks away, a small brick building with a narrow front yard and a wooden porch.

She stood on the porch for a moment, her hand resting on the railing. The house felt quiet, almost expectant. She unlocked the door and stepped inside.

The air smelled faintly of old books and lavender. The living room was exactly as she remembered — the armchair by the window, the crocheted blanket draped over the back, the bookshelf filled with Greek novels and history books. She ran her fingers along the spines, wishing she could read them.

She walked through the house slowly, taking in every detail. The kitchen still had the ceramic bowl her grandfather used for olives. The hallway still had the framed photograph of Lefkada he had hung decades ago. The bedroom still had the quilt her grandmother had made before she passed.

Daphne sat on the edge of the bed and closed her eyes. She felt a wave of emotion wash over her — grief, longing, regret, love. She wished she could talk to him one more time. She wished she could tell him she was learning Greek. She wished she could ask him about the treasure.

She opened her eyes and looked around the room. She noticed a small wooden box on the nightstand. She picked it up and opened it. Inside was a collection of old photographs — black-and-white images of her grandfather as a young man, standing on a beach, sitting on a boat, smiling with friends.

She held one of the photographs up to the light. Her grandfather stood on a cliff overlooking the sea, his hair tousled by the wind, his expression serene. Behind him, the water stretched out in endless shades of blue.

She felt inspired and determined. She would go to Lefkada. She would follow the clues. She would find whatever he had left for her.

She placed the photographs back in the box, closed it gently, and stood. She walked through the house one last time, taking in every detail, then walked towards the door.

As she was about to leave, she paused in the doorway. Something tugged at her — a small, familiar ache she couldn't quite name. She turned back toward the kitchen, drawn by the sudden urge to breathe in the scent of his Greek coffee one more time. It had always lingered in the air here, rich and earthy, clinging to the walls long after the cup was empty.

She stepped inside and opened the upper cabinet where he kept the small copper *briki* and the packets of finely ground coffee. The smell rose immediately — warm, bittersweet, unmistakably him. She closed her eyes for a moment, letting it settle around her like a memory.

When she opened them again, she noticed something tucked behind the coffee tins. A white envelope, slightly bent at the corner, as if it had been pushed out of sight in a hurry. She reached for it, her fingers brushing the textured lining of the shelf.

The return address was stamped in blue ink:

ASTORIA HISTORICAL SOCIETY
36-01 30th Avenue, Queens, NY

Her grandfather's name was typed neatly on the front.

Daphne hesitated before sliding the letter out. The paper inside was crisp, the tone polite and formal. They thanked him for "sharing copies of his notes regarding the mechanical device" and expressed interest in "continuing the conversation at his convenience." At the bottom, the director had added a handwritten line:

We would love to learn more about your work. Please visit us anytime.

Daphne read the letter twice, her pulse quickening. Her grandfather had never mentioned corresponding with the Historical Society. He had never mentioned "notes," either — or any kind of project that would interest a museum. She looked around the small kitchen, suddenly aware of how many things she didn't know about him.

She folded the letter carefully and put it in her purse. Whatever he had been working on, the Historical Society knew something about it. And now, she needed to know too.

As she walked home, she felt a sense of clarity she hadn't felt in weeks. She knew what she needed to do. She knew where she needed to go.

CHAPTER 4

Daphne had always believed that grief moved in straight lines. You felt the shock, then the sadness, then the acceptance, and eventually you reached a place where the memories softened and the ache dulled. But the weeks after her grandfather's death taught her that grief was more like a tide — unpredictable, shifting, sometimes gentle, sometimes overwhelming. One moment she felt steady, and the next she was swept under by a wave of longing so strong it left her breathless.

Yet beneath the grief, something else had begun to take shape. A quiet determination. A sense of purpose. A feeling that her grandfather had left her not just a letter, but a path.

She followed that path in small steps at first — studying Greek, revisiting his house, rereading the letter. But each step brought her closer to a truth she could feel but not yet name.

The following Saturday morning, Daphne slipped the letter from the Astoria Historical Society into the inside pocket of her coat and stepped out into the cool Astoria air. The sky was pale and cloudless, the kind of early-morning blue that made everything feel sharper, more possible. She walked with purpose, her hands tucked into her sleeves, the envelope pressing lightly against her chest with each step. She hadn't been able to stop thinking about it since she found it tucked behind the coffee tins.

Copies of his notes regarding the mechanical device. Continuing the conversation at his convenience. They would love to learn more about his work.

Work she had never heard of. A "mechanical device" that she had never seen.

Her grandfather had been many things — stubborn, private, tender in his own quiet way — but he had never been secretive. Or at least she had never thought so. Now, walking down 30th Avenue with the morning sun warming her shoulders, she wasn't so sure.

The Astoria Historical Society came into view at the corner, its brick façade softened by ivy and the faint glow of the early light. It was a small building tucked between a laundromat and a hardware store, easy to miss unless you knew it was there. Daphne paused at the steps, her breath catching for a moment. She wasn't sure what she expected to find inside — answers, maybe. Or more questions. But the director's handwritten note had lodged itself in her mind like a small, insistent bell.

If her grandfather had been in contact with them... If he had shared notes about something he never told her... If he had been working on a project important enough for a museum to follow up...

Then this was the only place to start.

The lobby of the Astoria Historical Society was quiet when Daphne stepped inside, the kind of quiet that felt intentional — a hush that belonged to old photographs, careful archives, and stories waiting to be uncovered. The air smelled faintly of paper and lemon polish. A volunteer at the front desk looked up from a stack of pamphlets and offered a polite smile.

"Good morning. Can I help you?"

"Yes," Daphne said, her fingers brushing the envelope in her coat pocket. "I... think so. I'm looking for someone who might know about a letter my grandfather received from here."

The volunteer's expression brightened with recognition of a familiar task. "You'll want the archives. Down the hall, second door on the left."

"Thank you."

Daphne walked down the narrow hallway, her footsteps soft against the old wooden floor. The door to the archives was propped open, and inside she found a woman in her sixties sorting through a box of photographs. She wore reading glasses on a chain and had the calm, focused air of someone who spent her days in the company of the past.

"Hello?" Daphne said gently.

The woman looked up. "Good morning. Come in."

Daphne stepped inside, suddenly aware of how tightly she was holding the envelope. "I'm sorry to bother you. My name is Daphne. My grandfather lived in Astoria for most of his life. I found a letter he received from this place, and I was hoping someone here might know what it was about."

The archivist set the photographs aside and gestured to a chair. "Let's take a look."

Daphne handed her the envelope. The woman adjusted her glasses and read the return address, then slid out the letter. Her eyes moved across the page with practiced ease.

"Ah," she murmured. "This is from our director. He retired last year, but I remember this correspondence."

Daphne leaned forward. "You do?"

"Yes." The woman looked up, straight into Daphne's eyes. "You said you found this letter. And you didn't ask your grandfather about it but came here instead. Does this mean that your grandfather…"

"He passed away," interrupted Daphne.

"Oh, I'm very sorry to hear that," the archivist said. "He was a very kind man. I remember him well. He came in several times. He brought us some notes — sketches, diagrams, bits of writing — about a mechanical device he was working on. Something he said he'd been building for years."

Daphne's breath caught. "He never told me about any of that."

The archivist gave her a sympathetic smile. "People keep their projects close to the chest sometimes. Especially if they're personal."

"What kind of device was it?" Daphne asked.

The woman hesitated, thoughtful. "I believe it was a replica of an Ancient Greek device, whose name escapes me at the moment. It seemed very complex. He said it was something he'd been trying to finish for a long time."

Daphne felt a small shiver run through her. "Do you still have the notes?"

"We made copies," the archivist said. "He took the originals back with him. But I can check the file."

She stood and crossed to a tall metal cabinet, sliding open a drawer with a soft metallic sigh. She flipped through folders with practiced efficiency until she found one labeled **Ioannis Papadakis - Mechanism Notes**.

Daphne's heart thudded.

The archivist opened the folder on the table. Inside were photocopies of pages in her grandfather's handwriting —

neat, careful script she recognized instantly. Some pages were filled with sketches: gears, levers, a circular frame. Others contained short paragraphs, fragments of thought, measurements, and questions.

Daphne leaned over the table, her breath shallow. "I had no idea he was working on anything like this." She traced a finger lightly above one of the sketches — a ring of interlocking gears, labeled in Greek.

"Do you know what it does?" she asked.

The archivist shook her head. "Not exactly. He spoke about it in metaphors. Something about time and the skies. He said it was inspired by an old device from an island in Greece."

Daphne's pulse quickened. "Did he say which island? Lefkada, perhaps?"

"No, I don't think so. He did mention Lefkada several times, though. That's where he came from, right?"

"Yes, he was from Lefkada," confirmed Daphne.

"I remember him saying that it was a place full of secrets."

Daphne's breath caught. "Secrets?"

The woman chuckled. "Not in a dramatic way. He meant history. Layers of it. He said the island held stories that people had forgotten."

This sounded very cryptic to Daphne, but she knew that the archivist was probably not the best person to ask for details about the secrets and the stories of Lefkada. She wished her grandfather had told her more about the island and its stories while he was alive.

The woman interrupted her thoughts. "What was the name of that island… Oh, even if I could remember, I'm sure I wouldn't be able to pronounce it. It was a difficult name, like most Greek names, I suppose," the archivist said and chuckled again.

"Is there anything else in the file?" asked Daphne.

The archivist flipped through the remaining pages. "Just a note from the director asking him to come back and explain more. He said he would come back with his notebook and a preliminary design. He never did."

Daphne sat back, absorbing the weight of that. Her grandfather had been working on something — something intricate, something meaningful — and he had kept it entirely to himself. Or maybe he had been waiting for the right moment to share it. But there was a notebook and a preliminary design. Where were those things? She needed to go back to her grandfather's house and search for them.

The archivist closed the folder gently. "You're welcome to take photos of these pages if you'd like. They belong to your family as much as they do to our records."

"Thank you," Daphne said, her voice soft.

She took out her phone and photographed each page carefully, her hands steady even as her heart raced. When she finished, she slipped the phone back into her pocket and looked at the archivist.

"Do you know why he stopped coming?"

The woman shook her head. "No. But he seemed… tired, the last time I saw him. As if he was carrying something heavy."

Daphne felt her throat tighten. A quiet breath escaped her — half-sorrow, half-ache. She stood slowly. "Thank you. Truly."

"You're welcome," the archivist said. "If you need anything else, feel free to come back."

Daphne nodded, the envelope warm in her pocket, the weight of her grandfather's secret work settling into her chest.

As she stepped back out into the bright morning, she felt something shift inside her — a small click, like the turning of a gear. Whatever her grandfather had been building, it wasn't finished. And now, she knew she had to follow where it led.

That evening, during her lesson with Tasos, she found herself unusually quiet. She listened intently, took notes, and repeated phrases, but her mind kept drifting back to the box at the historical society.

At the end of the lesson, Tasos tilted his head. "You seem distracted today."

"I'm okay," she said. "Just thinking about my grandfather."

He nodded sympathetically. "Grief takes time. Be patient with yourself."

She hesitated, then asked, "Do you know much about Ancient Greek inventions or mechanical devices?"

Tasos blinked, surprised. "Not much, just a few things I learned in school. I can tell you about the Phaistos Disk, it's a fascinating piece of history. Why do you ask?"

"No reason," she said quickly. "Just curious."

"There's another device I remember learning about in school. The Antikythera mechanism. A very intricate mechanical device."

The Antikythera mechanism. Daphne froze. Could that be the name the archivist at the Historical Society couldn't pronounce? She said her grandfather was building a replica. Could it be a replica of the Antikythera mechanism?

Tasos continued, "It's one of the oldest known mechanical devices. A corroded bronze mechanism recovered from a shipwreck. Thousands of years old, yet astonishingly complex. Some people call it the world's first computer."

Daphne felt a shiver. "Really?"

"Yes. It tracked the movements of the sun, moon, and planets. It predicted eclipses. It was incredibly advanced for its time."

Daphne remembered the archivist's words, "something about time and the skies". This was it, she was certain.

"A remarkable artifact," continued Tasos. "I feel ashamed, though, because I should know much more about it. I'll read about it and I'll be able to tell you more in our next lesson, I promise."

After the lesson ended, Daphne sat at her desk and looked for information on the Antikythera mechanism. She started to read the first page that came up. "Do you really expect me to understand this, Papou?" she said out loud, discouraged. She closed that page and opened a map of Lefkada. She printed it out and studied it carefully. She imagined the roads, the villages, the cliffs. She wondered where her grandfather's house was. She wondered what he had hidden there. She wondered why he had chosen her. Feeling overwhelmed, she appreciated the timely interruption of her thoughts when her phone rang. It was her friend Elena, asking her to go to their favorite coffee shop. Daphne was grateful for the excuse to get out of the house for a couple of hours.

They sat at a small table outside a café, the sun warming their faces. Elena stirred her latte thoughtfully.

"You've been quiet lately," Elena said. "Everything okay?"

Daphne hesitated. She wanted to tell Elena everything —
about the letter, the mechanism, the treasure. But she
couldn't. Her grandfather had been clear. The letter was
for her eyes only.

"I've just been busy," Daphne said. "Work, family stuff,
learning Greek."

Elena raised an eyebrow. "Greek? Since when?"

"Since a few weeks ago," Daphne said. "I'm taking
lessons."

"That's amazing," Elena said. "What made you decide to
start now?"

Daphne took a sip of her coffee. "My grandfather always
wanted me to learn. I guess I finally realized how much it
meant to him."

Elena smiled. "He would be proud."

Daphne felt a pang of emotion. "I hope so."

They talked about lighter things after that — work, books,
weekend plans — but Daphne's mind kept drifting back
to the letter. She felt a growing urgency, a sense that time
was moving faster than she could keep up with. Instead of
going back home, she decided to visit her grandfather's
house again. She walked through the quiet streets, the air
crisp and cool. When she reached the house, she unlocked
the door and stepped inside.

The living room was bathed in soft morning light. Dust motes floated in the air, drifting lazily. She walked to the bookshelf and pulled out a few of the Greek novels her grandfather had loved. She couldn't read them yet, but she held them carefully, feeling the weight of their stories.

She moved to the desk in the corner, where her grandfather had spent countless hours reading, writing, and tinkering with mechanical puzzles. She opened the drawers, finding pens, notebooks, and small tools. In the bottom drawer, she found a wooden box.

She lifted it onto the desk and opened it. Inside was a small metal object wrapped in cloth. She unwrapped it carefully, revealing a metal cylinder with engraved markings. Her breath caught.

She turned it over in her hand, studying the markings. She wondered if they were astronomical symbols — phases of the moon, perhaps, or zodiac signs. She felt a thrill of recognition. Her grandfather had been working on something connected to the Antikythera mechanism. Could this be a piece of it?

She placed the cylinder gently on the desk and opened the notebook that was under the box in the drawer. It was full of sketches and notes, which didn't surprise her. She compared the sketches to the cylindrical piece but found no similarities. She closed the notebook and put it in her bag along with the cylinder, her mind racing. She needed to go to Greece. She needed to follow the clues. She needed to find the treasure. Would the treasure be connected to the notes, to the cylindrical piece, to the Antikythera mechanism? Perhaps to all of the above?

When she arrived home, she immediately turned on her computer to search for the Antikythera mechanism again. She studied the images, comparing them to the sketches in her grandfather's notebook. The resemblance was unmistakable. She wondered how long he had been studying the mechanism. She wondered if he had ever seen the original in the museum. She still could not find any drawing of the cylinder, though, and she started to feel frustrated. Why did her grandfather have to be so cryptic? Did he really expect her to understand his notes? Or were the notes never meant for her, but only the letter? What was the "treasure"? She needed to go to Lefkada as soon as possible and look for whatever it was that she was supposed to find. But she also knew she needed to be prepared. She needed to understand the language, the culture, the history. She needed to be ready for whatever she would discover.

That evening her mother had invited her for dinner but she preferred to stay at home and eat alone. She prepared some scrambled eggs and sat at her kitchen table with the letter, the notebook, and the cylinder laid out in front of her. She studied them carefully again, waiting for a connection to jump out of the words or the drawings. She recognized more words in the letter now — enough to sense that her grandfather had written about something old, something hidden, something precious.

She whispered some words aloud, letting the sounds settle in her mind. She didn't know when she would go to Greece. She didn't know how she would find the treasure. But she knew she would.

She finished her dinner, closed the notebook, placed the cylinder beside it, and went to bed, hoping that her grandfather would send her some clues in her dreams.

CHAPTER 5

Daphne woke earlier than usual, long before the sun had fully risen. The sky outside her window was a muted gray, the kind of color that made the world feel suspended between night and day. She lay still for a moment, listening to the faint hum of traffic in the distance and the soft creak of her radiator. Her mind was already alert, filled with thoughts of her grandfather's notebook, the cylinder she had found in his drawer, and the map of Lefkada lying on her kitchen table like an invitation.

She had never been someone who thrived on uncertainty. She liked plans, schedules, lists. She liked knowing what came next. But lately, she felt as if she were standing at the edge of something vast and unknown, and instead of fear, she felt a strange sense of anticipation. It was as if her grandfather had left a trail of breadcrumbs, and she was finally ready to follow them.

She got out of bed, made coffee, and sat at her kitchen table. She looked at the map of Lefkada again. She wondered which part of the island held the house he had mentioned in the letter. She wondered if it still stood, or if time had worn it down to ruins. She wondered what he had hidden there, and why he had chosen her to find it.

She opened the notebook and flipped to the page with the diagram of the mechanism. The gears interlocked with precise symmetry, each one essential to the movement of the whole. She studied the lines carefully, trying to imagine how the pieces fit together. She didn't understand the mechanics, but she felt drawn to the design, as if it held a message she was meant to decipher.

Her grandfather had always loved puzzles. He used to give her wooden brainteasers when she was a child, encouraging her to think creatively. "There's always a solution," he would say. "You just have to look at the problem from the right angle."

She wondered if the letter was his final puzzle.

She closed the notebook and leaned back in her chair. She felt a mixture of excitement and frustration. She was making progress, but not fast enough.

Her phone buzzed, breaking her concentration. It was a message from her mother.

Thinking of you today. Hope you're doing okay.

Daphne typed a quick reply, then set the phone aside. She appreciated her mother's concern, but she didn't want to talk about her grief. And she certainly didn't want to talk about the letter.

She stood and walked to her bookshelf, scanning the titles. She pulled out a book on Greek history her grandfather had given her when she was a teenager. "It's a reminder," he had said, "that our ancestors understood more than we give them credit for." She remembered reading it halfheartedly at the time, more interested in the illustrations than the stories. Now, she opened it with a sense of reverence.

She flipped through the pages, stopping at a chapter about ancient inventions. There was a brief mention of the Antikythera mechanism, accompanied by a small illustration. She read it quickly, then closed the book and returned it to the shelf. She felt a growing sense of urgency. She needed to learn more — not just about the language, but about the island. She needed to understand the context of the clues her grandfather had left.

She grabbed her coat and headed outside. The air was cool, carrying the scent of roasted chestnuts from a street vendor. She walked briskly, her mind racing. She didn't have a destination in mind, but her feet carried her toward the Greek bookstore on Steinway Street.

The shop was small and cozy, with shelves packed tightly together and a faint smell of old paper lingering in the air. A bell chimed as she entered, and the owner, a middle-aged man with kind eyes, looked up from behind the counter.

"Kalimera," he said with a smile.

"Kalimera," Daphne replied, feeling a small thrill at repeating the greeting.

"Looking for something in particular?" he asked.

"I'm learning Greek," she said. "And I'm trying to learn more about Greece. Especially the Ionian islands."

The owner nodded thoughtfully. "We have a few books that might interest you."

He led her to a shelf near the back of the store and pulled out a thick volume with a bronze-colored cover. It was titled "Greek islands then and now."

"I would recommend this one," he said. "Very detailed. It covers many of the islands and their history."

Daphne felt her pulse quicken. "I'll take it."

She paid for the book and tucked it into her bag. As she walked home, she felt a renewed sense of purpose. She wasn't just learning Greek anymore. She was connecting to the culture. She was uncovering a story — her grandfather's story, and perhaps her own.

When she reached her apartment, she made tea and settled onto the couch with the book. She wasn't surprised to find a chapter dedicated to Lefkada. She began reading right away. The text was dense, filled with historical references, but she absorbed as much as she could. She learned about the ancient settlements, the Venetian influence, the beautiful landscapes."

She imagined her grandfather living there, and she pictured herself walking the same narrow streets. She closed the book and rested her head against the back of the couch. She felt a deep ache in her chest — not just grief, but longing. She wished she could talk to him. She wished she could ask him why he had chosen her. She wished she could tell him she was trying.

Her phone buzzed again. This time, it was a message from Tasos.

Hope your studies are going well. Let me know if you want extra practice this week.

She smiled. She appreciated his support more than she expected. She typed a reply.

I'd like that. I'm trying to make faster progress.

He responded almost immediately.

We can schedule something tomorrow. Just tell me what time works for you.

She felt a warm flutter in her chest. She wasn't sure if it was gratitude, admiration, or something else entirely. She pushed the thought aside and focused on the task at hand.

She opened her notebook and wrote a new sentence at the top of a fresh page:

Follow the clues.

She underlined it twice.

She spent the rest of the afternoon studying, flipping between the book, the notebook, and the letter. She practiced reading Greek aloud, sounding out each word carefully. She compared the vocabulary in the letter to the words in her lessons, searching for connections. She studied the diagrams in the notebook, trying to understand their significance.

As the sun began to set, she stood and stretched. Her mind felt full, but in a satisfying way. She walked to the window and looked out at the street below. The lights of the city glowed softly, casting a warm hue over the buildings. She felt a sense of calm settle over her.

The next morning arrived with a pale wash of sunlight that crept slowly across Daphne's bedroom floor. She lay still for a moment, letting the quiet settle around her. The city outside was just beginning to stir, but inside her apartment, everything felt suspended — as if the world were waiting for her to take the next step.

She rose, made coffee, and returned to the kitchen table where the map of Lefkada still lay open. The edges had begun to curl slightly from how often she had unfolded and refolded it. She smoothed it with her palm, tracing the coastline with a slow, deliberate motion. The island felt closer now, not just a place on a map but a destination with gravity, pulling her toward it.

She opened her grandfather's notebook again, flipping through the pages. The sketches were meticulous, each line drawn with care. She studied the interlocking gears, the circular dials, the notations in the margins. She didn't understand the mechanics, but she recognized the intention behind the drawings — the desire to preserve something ancient, to honor a piece of history that had fascinated him for decades.

She wondered when he had begun working on these drawings. She suspected he had built something based on them. But if he had, where was it now? It couldn't possibly be in Lefkada, her grandfather hadn't returned to the island since he left. Could it be in his house? Should she go back and look more carefully? She wondered if he had ever shown it to anyone. She doubted it. Her grandfather had always been private about his projects, sharing only the finished results, never the process.

She closed the notebook and leaned back in her chair. She felt a familiar ache in her chest — the ache of missing him, of wanting to ask him questions she would never be able to ask. She wished she could sit with him one more time, listening to him talk about the stars, the sea, the island where he had grown up. She wished she could tell him she was finally learning Greek, finally following the path he had hoped she would take.

Her phone buzzed, pulling her from her thoughts. It was a message from Tasos.

Let me know what time works for our extra lesson today.

She typed a quick reply, choosing a time in the late afternoon. She wanted to spend the morning studying on her own, reviewing vocabulary and practicing pronunciation. She wanted to feel prepared.

She spent the next few hours immersed in her lessons. She repeated phrases aloud, wrote sentences in her notebook, and listened to recordings of native speakers. She felt a small thrill each time she recognized a word from the letter. She was still far from understanding the full message, but the fragments were beginning to form a pattern.

Around noon, she took a break and walked to the park. The air was cool, and the trees swayed gently in the breeze. She found an empty bench and sat down, watching children play on the swings and couples stroll along the path. She felt a sense of calm settle over her.

She pulled the letter from her bag and unfolded it. The paper was soft from handling. She read the first line slowly, sounding out each word. She recognized more than she had the week before. She recognized references to a house, to something hidden, to a journey she was meant to take.

She whispered the words aloud, letting the sounds settle in her mind. She felt a quiet thrill — not just because she was learning, but because she was connecting with her grandfather in a way she never had before. The language felt like a bridge between them, spanning the distance created by time and loss.

Towards the middle of the page, she read the word "γραφείο". She had seen it before but couldn't remember its meaning. She remembered "γράφω" – to write. Could it be related? She repeated it a few times, "γραφείο". "Office!" she exclaimed, startling a woman who happened to be walking her dog past Daphne's bench. What office could her grandpa be referring to? Would she have to go to some office in Greece? Perhaps it was a specific type of office. She couldn't wait for her lesson in a few hours, to ask Tasos .

She folded the letter carefully and returned it to her bag. She sat for a few more minutes, watching the sunlight filter through the leaves. She felt a sense of clarity she hadn't felt in days.

When she returned home, she prepared for her lesson with Tasos. She set up her laptop, arranged her notebook and pen, and took a deep breath. When the call rang, she clicked "Accept."

Tasos appeared on the screen, smiling warmly. "Hello, Daphne. Ready for some extra practice?"

"Yes," she said. "Let's do this!"

"Let's start with some new vocabulary and then move on to some sentences," Tasos said.

"All right. Oh, Tasos, does 'γραφείο' mean 'office'? I saw the word in a book today."

"Yes! Good job!" Tasos exclaimed, proud of his student. And then he continued, "It also means 'desk'. It comes from the verb 'γράφω', which means 'to write'."

Daphne froze, her heart pounding. She was certain that her grandfather was referring to his desk. He wanted her to look in his desk, which she already had.

"Tasos, how do you say 'drawer'?"

"Το συρτάρι," he replied. "I know that's a hard one to pronounce, but let's give it a try. "Συρτάρι," he said slowly. Daphne repeated the word, her "rho" still not properly rolled. She would look for this word in the letter right after today's lesson.

They continued with vocabulary and then moved on to simple sentences, as Tasos had suggested. Daphne repeated each phrase carefully, focusing on the rhythm and intonation. Tasos corrected her gently when she slipped, offering encouragement with every improvement.

After an hour, he leaned back in his chair. "You're progressing quickly," he said. "You're putting in the work."

"I want to understand more," she said. "I feel like I'm getting closer."

He nodded. "Language opens doors. Sometimes to places we didn't expect."

After the lesson ended, Daphne grabbed the letter. She didn't even have to look hard. There it was, a couple of words after the word "γραφείο". "Στο γραφείο μου, στο τρίτο συρτάρι" – In my desk, in the third drawer. She felt a renewed sense of accomplishment. She was making progress — it felt must faster now — and she knew she was moving in the right direction.

She spent the rest of the afternoon studying. As evening approached, she stood and stretched. Her mind felt full, but in a satisfying way. She walked to the window and looked out at the street below. The lights of the city glowed softly, casting a warm hue over the buildings. A wave of calm washed over her, mingling with a surge of excitement.

She didn't know exactly where this journey would lead. She didn't know what she would find in Lefkada. She didn't know what secrets her grandfather had left behind. But she knew she was ready to take the next step. She was ready to book her trip.

CHAPTER 6

Daphne had always imagined that booking a flight to another country would feel exhilarating — a bold declaration of independence, a leap into the unknown. Instead, when she finally sat down at her laptop to choose her dates for Greece, she felt a tightness in her chest that had nothing to do with excitement. Her cursor hovered over the "Confirm Purchase" button for nearly a full minute before she forced herself to click it.

The confirmation email appeared instantly, bright and official. She stared at it, her pulse quickening. She was going to Greece. She was actually going.

The realization washed over her in a wave of conflicting emotions — anticipation, fear, curiosity, longing, and above all, anxiety. She closed her laptop and pressed her palms against her eyes, trying to steady her breathing. She had wanted this. She had worked toward it. She had studied, prepared, and followed every clue her grandfather had left. But now that the trip was real, her mind began to spin with possibilities she hadn't allowed herself to consider.

What if she got sick on the plane? What if she caught something in the airport? What if she needed medicine she didn't have? What if she had an allergic reaction to something unfamiliar? What if she touched a surface that hadn't been cleaned properly?

The thoughts came quickly, one after another, like a cascade she couldn't stop. She stood abruptly and walked to the kitchen, opening the cabinet where she kept her first-aid supplies. She pulled out a box of disinfecting wipes, then another, then a bottle of antibacterial spray. She placed them on the counter in a neat row.

She opened another cabinet and retrieved a small plastic bin filled with medications — allergy pills, cold tablets, cough drops, eye drops, nose spray, bandages, ointments. She emptied the bin onto the counter, sorting everything into categories. She made a list of what she needed to restock. She added items she didn't technically need but felt safer having — throat lozenges, motion sickness tablets, extra bandages, a small thermometer.

She knew she was overdoing it. She knew most people didn't pack half a pharmacy for a two-week trip. But the idea of being unprepared made her stomach twist. She needed to feel in control. She needed to know she could handle whatever came her way.

She took a deep breath and began packing the items into a small travel pouch. She arranged everything carefully, making sure each item was visible and accessible. She added a second pouch for disinfecting supplies. She placed both pouches in her suitcase, then stood back and surveyed her work.

It wasn't enough.

She opened her laptop again and ordered travel-size sanitizing wipes, a portable UV sterilizer, and a pack of disposable gloves. She added a small bottle of hand sanitizer to her cart, then another, then a third. She hesitated before checking out, but the thought of running out mid-flight made her skin prickle.

When the order was confirmed, she closed her laptop and exhaled slowly. She felt slightly calmer, though the knot in her stomach remained.

She walked to her desk and opened her grandfather's letter. She read the first few paragraphs, sounding out the Greek words carefully. She recognized more than she had the week before. She recognized references to something hidden, to a piece that needed to be brought to the island. She recognized the word "τοποθέτησε," place it. She recognized "τελευταίο κομμάτι," final piece.

Her breath caught.

She looked at the small cylinder she had found in her grandfather's drawer. It sat on her desk, gleaming faintly in the afternoon light. She picked it up and turned it over in her hand. The markings were intricate, the craftsmanship precise. She felt a shiver run through her.

This was the missing piece. The letter wasn't just telling her to go to Lefkada. It was telling her to bring this with her.

She placed the cylinder gently back on the desk and reread the section of the letter that mentioned the mechanism. She looked for the word "Αντικύθηρα" – Antikythera, but could not find it anywhere. She read that section again. She recognized enough words to understand the gist — the device would not function without the final piece. What she had to do seemed to be clearly explained, though she couldn't yet understand all the details. She would need help. She would need someone who could translate the letter fully, someone who could guide her through the process. She thought of Tasos. He had been patient, encouraging, and unexpectedly kind. He had helped her navigate the language, the culture, the history. He had answered her questions without judgment, even when she stumbled. She trusted him. She needed him.

She opened the tutoring platform and sent him a message.

Hi Tasos, I booked my flight to Greece. I'll be arriving in a few weeks. I might need some help when I get there.

She hesitated before sending it, unsure how much to reveal. She didn't want to overwhelm him. She didn't want to sound needy. But she also didn't want to face the journey alone.

She hit "Send" before she could second-guess herself.

She spent the rest of the afternoon preparing for the trip. She made a packing list, then revised it twice. She checked the airline's baggage policy. She researched travel health tips. She read articles about staying safe on long flights. She watched videos about disinfecting airplane seats.

By evening, she felt mentally exhausted. She sat on the couch and closed her eyes, letting the quiet settle around her. She tried to imagine herself on the plane, breathing calmly, feeling steady. She tried to imagine herself stepping onto Greek soil, feeling the warmth of the sun, hearing the language she had been studying for months. She tried to imagine the house in Lefkada — the house her grandfather had written about, the house that held the rest of the mechanism.

Her phone buzzed. She opened it and saw a message from Tasos.

That's wonderful news, Daphne. I'm happy for you. And of course I'll help. Just tell me when you arrive.

She felt a warmth spread through her chest. She typed a reply.

Thank you. I'll send you the details soon.

She set her phone aside and stood, stretching her arms above her head. She walked to her desk and picked up the cylinder again. She held it carefully, feeling its weight, its coolness, its significance.

She imagined the mechanism in Lefkada — silent, incomplete, waiting. She imagined placing the final piece into its slot, hearing the first click of movement, watching the gears turn. She imagined her grandfather standing beside her, smiling with quiet pride.

She placed the cylinder gently into a small velvet pouch and tucked it into her carry-on bag. She zipped the bag closed and placed it beside her suitcase.

She walked to the window and looked out at the city. The lights glowed softly, casting a warm hue over the buildings. She knew that she would soon be in a place that looked nothing like this.

The days that followed were a blur of preparation, anticipation, and a steady undercurrent of anxiety that Daphne tried — and failed — to ignore. Her flight was now less than two weeks away, and every morning she woke with the same thought: *I'm really doing this.*

She had never traveled alone before. She had never flown overseas. She had never been to a foreign country where she barely spoke the language and where she didn't know anyone. The enormity of it pressed on her chest whenever she paused long enough to think. So she didn't pause. She prepared.

Her apartment slowly transformed into a staging area for the trip. Her suitcase lay open on the floor, half-packed with clothes, travel-size toiletries, and the growing collection of disinfecting supplies she kept adding to. The pouches of medicine sat neatly on her dresser, each one labeled with a sticky note. She had even created a small "in-flight emergency kit" containing hand sanitizer, wipes, tissues, six spare masks, and a tiny bottle of lavender oil she hoped might calm her nerves.

One afternoon, she sat on the floor surrounded by her packing lists. She had three versions — one handwritten, one typed, and one color-coded. She cross-checked them carefully, making sure she hadn't forgotten anything essential. She added a few more items: electrolyte packets, a small sewing kit, two cell-phone chargers, an adaptor, a pack of tissues infused with eucalyptus.

She paused, staring at the growing pile. *This is ridiculous,* she thought. No, she wouldn't let her hypochondria ruin this trip. She was over that. She had gone through countless online videos with tips and tricks about rewiring her brain. She needed to focus on her mission. Every time she thought she had a condition or infection or simply felt a minor ache anywhere in her body, it was the only thing she could think of all day. On those days, even if someone spoke to her, she would hear but not truly listen, and though she looked around, she did not really see. But now she was determined to be mentally strong and focus on her grandfather's wish. She put the masks back in the drawer, as well as all but one pack of sanitizing wipes. But what if the foldable table on the plane was disgusting? She took out one pack again. The hand sanitizer… she would think about it later, perhaps she would leave one or two of the four bottles she had prepared.

Her phone buzzed with a message from her mother.

Do you need help packing? I can come over.

Daphne stared at the message for a moment before replying.

I'm okay. Just trying to get organized.

Her mother responded with a heart emoji. Daphne set the phone aside and exhaled slowly. She didn't want her mother to see how anxious she was. She didn't want anyone to see it. She wanted to appear capable, confident, ready.

She stood and walked to her carry-on bag and took out the velvet pouch containing the cylinder. She took out the cylinder and held it in her palm. It felt cool and solid, grounding her in a way nothing else did. She traced the markings with her fingertip, imagining the mechanism waiting for it in the old house in Lefkada. She wondered what the device would look like assembled. She wondered how it would move, what sounds it would make, what secrets it would reveal. She wondered if her grandfather had ever seen it completed, or if he had left that moment for her.

She placed the cylinder back in the pouch. She tucked it into her carry-on bag again, making sure it was secure. She would not risk losing it. She would not let it out of her sight.

That evening, she had another lesson with Tasos. She sat at her desk, smoothing her hair and adjusting her webcam. When the call rang, she clicked "Accept."

Tasos appeared on the screen, smiling warmly. "Hello, Daphne. How are you feeling about your trip?"

"Nervous," she admitted. "Excited, but nervous."

"That's normal," he said. "Traveling to a new place can be overwhelming. But you'll be fine. Greece is welcoming."

She smiled faintly. "I hope so."

They began the lesson, focusing on travel-related vocabulary — airport phrases, directions, common questions. Daphne repeated each phrase carefully, trying to memorize the rhythm of the language. She stumbled a few times, but Tasos corrected her gently.

After an hour, he leaned back in his chair. "You're improving," he said. "You'll be able to communicate the basics."

"I'm trying," she said. "I want to be prepared."

"You will be," he said. "And if you need help when you arrive, I'll be there."

She felt a warmth spread through her chest. "Thank you. That means a lot."

They ended the call, and Daphne sat for a moment, staring at the blank screen. She felt a mixture of gratitude and something softer, something she didn't want to name yet.

She closed her laptop and headed to the bathroom to remove the makeup she had put on right before her lesson.

She walked to the window and looked out at the city. The lights glowed softly, casting a warm hue over the buildings. She felt a sense of calm settle over her.

The next morning, she woke with a renewed sense of purpose. She made coffee, sat at her kitchen table, and opened her grandfather's letter. She read the first few lines slowly, sounding out each word. She recognized more than she had the last time. In addition to references to a house, to something hidden, to a piece that needed to be brought to the island, now she had noticed the word "οικογένεια," family.

She paused, her breath catching. Why had he mentioned family in the same section as the mechanism? Why had he written about the house as if someone lived there? Why had he been so secretive?

She read the line again, tracing the letters with her fingertip. She didn't understand the full meaning yet, but she felt a flicker of unease. She sensed that the house in Lefkada held more than just the mechanism. She sensed that her grandfather had left more than one secret behind.

She closed the letter and placed it gently on the table. She stood and walked to her suitcase, adding a few more items — a travel pillow, a small blanket, a pack of sanitizing wipes she had forgotten she owned. She zipped the suitcase closed and sat on the edge of her bed, feeling a mixture of exhaustion and anticipation.

Her phone buzzed again. It was a message from her cousin Irene.

I heard you're going to Greece! That's amazing. Send pictures.

Daphne smiled and typed a reply.

I will. I'm excited.

I'm also terrified, she admitted to herself out loud.

CHAPTER 7

Daphne woke before her alarm, the room still dim and quiet. For a moment she lay still, listening to the faint hum of the radiator and the distant rumble of an early bus outside. Her mind was already alert. Today she would leave New York. Today she would cross an ocean. Today she would start carrying her grandfather's final instructions into the world.

She sat up slowly, letting the reality settle in. Her suitcase waited by the door, zipped and ready. Her carry-on bag sat beside it, the velvet pouch containing the metal cylinder tucked safely inside. She reached for the bag and unzipped the inner pocket, checking the pouch again even though she had checked it twice the night before. The gear felt cool and reassuring in her hand. She held it for a moment, tracing the engraved markings with her thumb, then slipped it back into the pouch and tightened the drawstring.

She would not risk losing it. Not in the airport. Not on the plane. Not anywhere.

She dressed, made a quick cup of coffee, and stood by the window while she drank it. The sky was still dark, but a faint glow hinted at the coming sunrise. She felt a mixture of nerves and determination settle in her chest. She had spent weeks preparing for this moment — studying Greek, deciphering the letter, gathering clues — and now the journey was finally beginning.

She grabbed her coat, locked the door behind her, and stepped into the hallway. The elevator ride felt strangely symbolic, as if she were descending from one chapter of her life into another. Outside, the air was crisp, and the street was quiet except for a few early commuters. She climbed into the cab she had booked the night before.

As the car pulled away, she watched the familiar streets pass by — the bakery where she bought her morning pastries, the café where she had spent hours reading, the grocery store where her grandfather used to insist on choosing his own produce. She felt a pang of nostalgia, but it was softened by the knowledge that she was following a path he had set for her.

The airport was already bustling when she arrived. She moved through the check-in line, her mind focused on the steps ahead — boarding pass, security, gate. She kept her carry-on bag close, her hand resting on the strap as if guarding something fragile. She didn't let herself think about the long flight or the unfamiliar country waiting on the other side. She focused on the next small task, then the next.

Security took longer than she expected, but she stayed calm. When the agent asked her to open her bag, she felt a flicker of panic, but the inspection was routine. The velvet pouch remained untouched. She zipped the bag closed and exhaled slowly.

At the gate, she found a seat near the window and watched the planes taxi across the runway. She felt a strange mixture of vulnerability and resolve. She was leaving everything familiar behind, but she wasn't running away. She was moving toward something — something she sensed was extremely important.

When her flight was called, she stood and joined the line. She stepped onto the plane, found her seat, and placed her carry-on bag under the seat in front of her. She touched the velvet pouch through the fabric, feeling the outline of the cylinder. She closed her eyes as the plane began to taxi. She didn't sleep, but she stayed steady.

Hours passed in a blur of movies, music, and quiet repetition of Greek phrases. She practiced simple sentences under her breath, imagining conversations she might have in Lefkada. She imagined asking for directions, ordering food, greeting strangers. She imagined standing in the old house, reading her grandfather's instructions aloud.

When the plane finally descended toward Athens, she felt a rush of relief. The city appeared below her — chaotic, with buildings too close to each other, narrow streets and small patches of green here and there. She pressed her forehead lightly against the window, taking in the view.

She had made it.

The airport was bright and busy, filled with voices speaking Greek, English, and languages she couldn't identify. She followed the signs to baggage claim, located the carousel for her flight and waited patiently for her bag. She wondered if Tasos was already waiting for her outside. Her heart was pounding with anticipation.

Her suitcase was one of the first ones to come out. She grabbed it from the carousel and walked towards the exit. The customs officers near the exit were too busy with a man who seemed to be carrying too many bottles of liquor. She kept going until she finally came out of the airport. She scanned the crowd, searching for a familiar face.

Then she saw him.

Tasos stood near a pillar, holding a small sign with her name written neatly across it. He looked exactly as he did on camera — warm eyes, easy smile — but somehow more grounded in person. When he spotted her, he lifted a hand in greeting.

"Daphne," he said as she approached. "Welcome to Greece."

Hearing her name in his voice made something inside her loosen. "Hi," she said, smiling despite her exhaustion. "Thank you for coming."

"Of course," he replied. "Let me help you with your bags."

The warm Greek air hit her immediately — softer, sweeter than the air back home. She inhaled deeply, feeling a strange sense of familiarity.

Tasos led her to his car and helped load her luggage. "Your hotel isn't far," he said. "You'll have time to rest."

She nodded, grateful. The exhaustion of the flight was beginning to settle into her bones.

As they drove through Athens, Daphne watched the city unfold around her — narrow streets, glimpses of ancient ruins rising unexpectedly between modern buildings. She felt a quiet thrill. She had seen pictures, but the real thing was different. More vivid. More alive.

"You'll like it here," Tasos said. "Athens has its own rhythm."

"It's beautiful," she said softly.

He smiled. "Tomorrow, if you're up for it, I can show you around a bit. Before you head to Lefkada."

She hesitated. "I don't want to take up your time."

"It's no trouble," he said. "And it's better than wandering alone your first day."

She felt a warmth spread through her chest. "I'd like that."

They reached her hotel, and Tasos helped her carry her bags inside. "Get some rest," he said. "I'll text you in the morning."

"Thank you," she said. "For everything."

He gave her a small nod and left.

Daphne checked into her room and set her bags down. She opened her carry-on and pulled out the velvet pouch. She placed it gently on the nightstand, then sat on the edge of the bed, letting the quiet settle around her.

She was here. She had made it. She lay back on the bed and closed her eyes. Sleep came quickly.

The next morning, Daphne woke to sunlight spilling across the hotel curtains. For a moment she didn't remember where she was. The room felt unfamiliar — the pale walls, the tiled floor, the faint hum of traffic outside. Then the memory returned in a warm rush: Athens. She was in Athens.

She sat up slowly, stretching her arms above her head. Her body felt heavy from the long flight, but her mind was alert. She checked the time — she had slept longer than she expected. Her phone buzzed with a message from Tasos.

Whenever you're ready, I'm downstairs. No rush.

She smiled. She appreciated that he didn't pressure her. She moved through her morning routine with deliberate calm — shower, clothes, makeup. She carefully grabbed the velvet pouch from her nightstand and put it in the inner zippered pocket of her purse. She wasn't going to risk leaving it in the hotel. She zipped the pocket closed and slung the bag over her shoulder.

When she stepped into the lobby, Tasos was waiting near the entrance, holding two coffees.

"Good morning," he said. "You look rested."

"I feel rested," she said. "Thank you for yesterday."

He handed her a cup. "Today will be easy. Just a walk, some food, a few places you might like."

They stepped outside, and the warmth of the morning wrapped around her. Athens felt different in daylight — brighter, louder, more alive. The streets buzzed with scooters, vendors, and people heading to work. The air carried the scent of coffee, exhaust, and something floral she couldn't identify.

Tasos led her through narrow streets lined with small shops. He pointed out bakeries, bookstores, and cafés tucked into corners she would have missed on her own.

Daphne listened, absorbing everything — the sounds, the colors, the rhythm of the city.

They stopped at a small café with tables spilling onto the sidewalk. Tasos ordered pastries filled with cheese, and they sat beneath a striped awning.

"This is the famous Greek *tyropita* that I mentioned so many times in our lessons," he explained. From *τυρί* – cheese and *πίτα* – pie."

"I know, I know. We have it in Astoria. My grandma used to make it too, but this tastes different. "More authentic— at least that's how it seems to me," Daphne said, laughing.

"I keep forgetting you live in a Greek neighborhood," Tasos said, sounding apologetic and nearly blushing.

Daphne loved his shyness. She took a bite of her pastry. It was warm, soft, and unexpectedly comforting. "I think I need that right now."

Tasos nodded. "You've had a lot on your mind."

She didn't answer. She didn't want to talk about the letter or the mechanism or the house waiting for her on the island. Not yet. She wanted to enjoy this moment — the sunlight, the food, the company.

After breakfast, they walked toward the historic center. The Acropolis rose above the city, its marble columns glowing in the sun. Daphne stopped, staring up at it.

"It's strange," she said quietly. "I've seen pictures my whole life, but this feels different."

"It always does," Tasos said. "It's one thing to look at history. It's another to stand in front of it."

They didn't climb the hill — Daphne didn't want to exhaust herself before the trip to Lefkada — but they walked through the surrounding streets, where ancient stones sat beside modern shops. She felt the weight of time everywhere, layered and alive.

At one point, they paused near a small square shaded by olive trees. Children played nearby, their laughter echoing off the buildings. Daphne watched them for a moment, feeling a tug of something she couldn't name.

"You're quiet," Tasos said gently.

"I'm thinking," she replied.

"About tomorrow?"

She nodded.

He didn't press. "Lefkada is peaceful," he said. "Whatever you're looking for, whether it's peace, relaxation, beautiful beaches, or good food, you'll find it there."

She appreciated that he didn't ask what exactly she was looking for. She wasn't ready to explain. She wasn't even sure she could. At the same time she felt a small tug of obligation to tell him the truth — not pressure, just the sense that she owed him something in return for all the kindness he had already shown her.

"I'm looking forward to all of that," she said softly, "but the main reason I'm going to Lefkada is to see my grandfather's homeland. And to visit the house where he grew up."

"That is a very good reason to visit Lefkada," Tasos said, his voice warm. "You are lucky to have ties to that island."

They continued walking until the afternoon heat grew heavy. Tasos suggested a break, and they found a shaded bench overlooking a small park. Daphne sat, sipping water, feeling the fatigue of travel settle into her limbs.

"You're handling everything well," Tasos said. "Most people are overwhelmed their first day."

"I'm trying to stay focused," she said. "There's a lot ahead."

He nodded. "I'll help you in any way I can."

She looked at him, surprised by the sincerity in his voice. "Thank you."

They sat in comfortable silence for a few minutes. Daphne watched the leaves rustle in the breeze, feeling a sense of calm she hadn't expected.

Eventually, Tasos stood. "Let's get you back to the hotel. You should rest before tomorrow."

She didn't argue. The day had been full — not rushed, but full enough to leave her pleasantly tired.

They walked back through the city, the afternoon sun casting long shadows across the streets. When they reached the hotel, Daphne turned to him.

"Today was wonderful," she said. "I'm glad we did this."

"Me too," he said. "Text me when you're ready tomorrow. I'll help you get to the bus station."

She hesitated. "You don't have to—"

"I want to," he said simply.

She felt a warmth spread through her chest. "Okay. I'll message you."

He gave her a small nod and walked away.

Daphne headed inside, took the elevator to her room, and closed the door behind her. The quiet felt different now — less lonely, more grounding. She set her bag on the bed and opened it, checking the velvet pouch again. The cylinder was still there, nestled safely inside.

She placed it on the nightstand and sat beside it. She traced the markings with her fingertip, imagining the mechanism waiting for it somewhere on the island. She imagined her grandfather writing the instructions, knowing she would one day follow them.

She repacked her bag, laid out clothes for the morning, and set her alarm. She got into bed and quickly fell asleep, worn out from the trip and the long walk in Athens.

Tomorrow, the real search would begin.

CHAPTER 8

Daphne woke before sunrise, the room still wrapped in shadows. For a moment she lay still, listening to the faint hum of the air conditioner and the distant murmur of traffic drifting up from the street. Her body felt heavy, but her mind was alert. Today she would leave Athens. Today she would reach her grandfather's island.

She sat up slowly and rubbed her eyes. The velvet pouch lay on the nightstand. She reached for it, feeling the familiar weight of the cylinder inside. She held it for a moment, letting its cool surface steady her, then slipped it into the inner pocket of her bag.

She dressed, checked her belongings twice, and headed downstairs. The lobby was quiet, the early hour giving everything a muted stillness. When she stepped outside, the air was warm and smelled faintly of coffee and warm bread drifting from a nearby bakery.

Tasos stood near the entrance, leaning casually against his car. He straightened when he saw her.

"Good morning," he said. "Ready for the next leg?"

"As ready as I'll ever be," she replied.

He opened the passenger door for her, and she climbed in. The city was just beginning to wake as they drove toward the bus station — shopkeepers lifting metal shutters, delivery trucks weaving through narrow streets, the sky shifting from gray to pale gold.

"You slept well?" Tasos asked.

"Better than I expected," she said. "Yesterday helped."

He smiled. "Athens has that effect on people."

They reached the station quickly. It was busier than Daphne anticipated — travelers with backpacks, families with suitcases. The air buzzed with conversation, announcements, and the hiss of engines.

Tasos parked and turned to her. "I'll help you get your ticket."

She followed him inside, grateful for his presence. The ticket counter was crowded, but Tasos navigated it with ease, speaking to the clerk in quick, fluid Greek. Within minutes, he handed her a ticket.

"You're all set," he said. "The bus leaves in twenty minutes."

Daphne looked at the printed slip, her stomach tightening. "Thank you. I don't think I could've figured that out on my own."

"You would have," he said. "But I'm glad I could make it easier."

They walked together. The bus was large and clean, with wide windows that promised a view of the countryside. Daphne felt a flutter of nerves.

"You'll be on the road for a while," Tasos said. "But the drive is beautiful. Mountains, sea, small towns. It's a good way to see the country."

She nodded, thankful that Lefkada was linked to the mainland by a bridge. The idea of traveling by boat frightened her, even though she'd remembered to bring dramamine just in case.

When the bus driver began loading luggage, Daphne handed over her suitcase. She kept her carry-on bag close, her hand resting on the strap.

Tasos noticed. "You're guarding that bag like it holds something priceless."

"It does," she said before she could stop herself.

He didn't press. "Then keep it close."

The bus door opened, and passengers began to board. Daphne turned to Tasos.

"Thank you," she said. "For everything."

"Don't mention it," he said. "It's been my pleasure. I mean it."

She hesitated, unsure what else to say. He gave her a small, reassuring smile.

"Text me when you arrive," he said. "I want to know you made it safely."

"I will," she promised.

She climbed onto the bus and found a seat by the window. As the engine rumbled to life, she looked out and saw Tasos still standing there, hands in his pockets. When he caught her eye, he lifted a hand in a small wave.

The bus pulled away, and he disappeared from view.

The city faded quickly, replaced by open roads and rolling hills. Daphne watched the landscape shift — olive groves stretching toward the horizon, clusters of houses perched on hillsides, glimpses of the sea flashing between trees. The scenery was so different from New York that it felt almost unreal.

She rested her forehead against the window, letting the rhythm of the bus soothe her. The hum of the engine, the soft murmur of passengers, the steady movement forward — it all created a sense of quiet momentum.

Hours passed. The bus stopped along the way at a rest area. Daphne stretched her legs, breathing in the scent of pine trees and sea air. She felt herself relaxing, the tension of travel slowly easing.

By early afternoon, the bus crossed the Agia Mavra bridge that connected Lefkada to the mainland. The water shimmered on both sides, bright and clear. Daphne leaned forward, her heart pounding.

She had reached the island.

The bus wound through narrow roads lined with cypress trees and stone walls. Villages appeared and disappeared — clusters of houses with red roofs, small squares shaded by plane trees, cafés with tables spilling onto the street. People moved with an ease that made Daphne feel like she had stepped into another world.

She checked the map her grandfather had sketched, tracing the route with her finger. The house was outside a village on the western side of the island. She would need to find a way to get there. Perhaps there was a bus, or perhaps she would need to take a taxi. She would need to figure it out, but first, she needed get to a guesthouse.

The thought made her stomach tighten, but she pushed the feeling aside. She had come this far. She could handle the rest.

The bus finally pulled into the station in Lefkada Town. Daphne gathered her things, slung her bag over her shoulder, and stepped outside. The air was warm and smelled faintly of salt and citrus. The sky was a brilliant blue.

She took a moment to steady herself, then walked toward the taxi stand. A few drivers stood nearby, chatting in Greek. One of them noticed her and approached.

"Πού πάτε;" he asked. Where are you going?

Daphne pulled out the map and pointed to the village. "Εδώ," she said. Here.

"Ah, Perigiali," the driver said confidently, motioning towards his car. She climbed in, her heart pounding again. The velvet pouch felt heavy in her bag.

"Πρώτη φορά στο νησί;" the driver asked with a friendly tilt of his head. First time on the island? "Ναι", Daphne replied, grateful for the warmth in his voice. She asked if there was a place in the village where she could stay the night, and his expression brightened. "Ναι, ναι—Pension Almyra. Just up the road from the village square. Clean rooms, good people. Do you want me to take you there?"

"Yes, that would be great," Daphne said, relieved that she would not have to look hard to find a place to stay.

As they drove through the island, Daphne watched the landscape unfold — cliffs rising above the sea, fields dotted with wildflowers, narrow roads winding through olive groves. The beauty of it was overwhelming.

But beneath the beauty, she felt something else — a quiet tension, a sense of being drawn toward something she couldn't yet see.

When the taxi reached the guesthouse, the driver slowed. "Εδώ είμαστε," he said. Here we are.

Daphne stepped out, a little nervous. The driver carried her suitcase to the guesthouse door. She gave him a generous tip and got inside.

Daphne stepped into the small guesthouse lobby, grateful for the cool shade after the heat outside. A woman at the reception desk looked up and greeted her with a warm smile.

"Hello, welcome," she said. "How can I help you?"

"I was hoping you might have a room available," Daphne said.

"Of course," the woman replied. "Where are you visiting from?"

"From the USA," Daphne said. "From New York."

The woman's face brightened. "From New York? All the way to our little village?" She reached for a set of keys hanging on a wooden board behind her. "Then you should have the room with the best view."

She placed the key in Daphne's hand with a friendly nod. "You'll see the sea from the balcony. It's beautiful in the evening."

"Thank you," Daphne said, touched by the unexpected kindness.

The guesthouse room was simple but charming — whitewashed walls, a small wooden wardrobe, a neatly made bed with a blue coverlet that reminded her of the sea. Everything looked clean enough, more than clean enough, actually. It had that crisp, sun-dried smell that only Greek linens seemed to have.

Still, the moment the door clicked shut behind her, Daphne felt the familiar prickle of unease crawl up her spine.

She set her bag down, exhaled, and then — almost automatically — reached for the packet of disinfecting wipes she always carried. She told herself it was just a precaution, just a quick once-over, nothing dramatic. But her hands were already moving with practiced efficiency.

First the door handle. Then the light switch. Then the faucet knobs, the sink edges, the toilet seat, the flush button, even the little metal latch on the bathroom window. She wiped each surface thoroughly, methodically, as if she were preparing an operating room rather than a guesthouse bathroom. The wipes made soft, determined swipes against the ceramic and metal, her movements quick and precise.

You're being reasonable, she told herself. *This is normal. People do this. Some people do this.*

But she knew — of course she knew — that most people didn't disinfect the underside of the faucet or the top of the toilet tank "just in case." Most people didn't pause halfway through wiping the shower knobs because they suddenly worried about airborne mold spores.

Her heart thudded a little too fast. Her breath caught in that familiar, irritating way.

It's fine, she whispered. *It's just a room. It's clean. You're fine.*

She finished the last surface, folded the used wipes into a neat little square, and dropped them into the trash. Only then did she straighten up, press her palms against her thighs, and take a steadying breath.

The room looked exactly the same as before — simple, tidy, welcoming — but now it felt safer. Or at least, safer *enough.*

And with everything finally clean, finally under control, she felt her body loosen. The tension in her shoulders eased. Her breath deepened. The knot in her stomach uncurled.

For the first time since arriving on the island, she felt calm.

She lay down on the bed, the blue coverlet cool beneath her cheek, and let her eyes drift shut. Disinfecting everything had given her the one thing she needed most — a sense of control, a sense of order, a sense that she could finally focus on the real reason she had come to Lefkada.

Within minutes, she was asleep.

She woke up at 1 a.m., not only because she had taken an absurdly long nap but also because the jet lag still clung to her like a weight she couldn't shake off. The room was silent, the village outside even quieter, and she lay there staring at the ceiling, wide awake. She was hungry, too — the kind of hollow, restless hunger that made it impossible to fall back asleep — but she had no food with her and nowhere to go at that hour. She kept glancing at the window, wishing morning would hurry up so she could finally get something to eat. What annoyed her most was the lost time. She had planned to look for the old house that afternoon, maybe even walk around the village a bit, but instead she had slept through the entire evening. Now she would have to wait until tomorrow.

She sat up and turned on the small lamp. If she couldn't sleep, she might as well prepare. She opened the map, tracing the route with her finger, trying to memorize the turns. She rehearsed how she would ask for directions if she couldn't find the house on her own — simple phrases, nothing complicated, just enough to get her there. The hours crawled by. At around four in the morning, her eyes finally grew heavy. Before lying down again, she set her alarm for 7 a.m., determined not to lose another day.

CHAPTER 9

Daphne woke before the sun had fully risen, the room still dim and washed in the soft gray of early morning. For a moment she didn't move. She lay still beneath the light blanket, listening to the faint sounds drifting through the open balcony door— a rooster crowing somewhere in the distance, the rustle of olive branches, the muted clatter of someone opening shutters down the street. The island was waking slowly, unhurried, as if it had all the time in the world.

She didn't.

Her mind was already racing.

She sat up, rubbing her eyes, and glanced around the small guesthouse room. The lavender sprig on the dresser had dried overnight, its scent faint but comforting. Her bag sat in the corner where she had left it, the map folded neatly on the bedside table. Everything looked exactly as it had last night, but she felt different — restless, unsettled, pulled forward by something she couldn't name.

Today she would go to the house.

She got dressed quickly and headed downstairs, determined not to lose any more time. She didn't bother asking the receptionist for a place to eat; she already knew where she was going. On the taxi ride in, she had spotted a small café on the village square, just a short walk from the guesthouse, and she had mentally bookmarked it. The square was still quiet at that early hour, but the café's lights were on, and the smell of baked pastries drifted out the door. She went straight to the counter, ordered a spanakopita to go, and added a frappé for good measure. She didn't want to sit, didn't want to linger—she just needed something in her stomach so she could get on with her day.

But eating was harder than she expected. She was starving, yet her nerves made every bite feel like a chore. She forced down the spanakopita in small, mechanical bites, the warm pastry turning heavy in her mouth. Even the frappé, cold and familiar, wasn't going down easily. She kept telling herself she needed the energy, that she couldn't afford to be shaky or unfocused when she finally went looking for the old house. Still, her stomach fluttered with that mix of hunger and anxiety she knew too well. She tossed the empty wrapper, took a breath, and told herself that once she started walking, everything would settle.

The village was small and quiet, with stone houses and narrow paths. She checked the map, trying to orient herself. The house appeared to be on the outskirts of the village, but the distance looked short; the whole place had seemed tiny during her taxi ride. She decided to try walking there. There didn't seem to be any buses, and she hadn't seen a single taxi on the streets. If necessary, she could call one, but she wanted to attempt the walk first. She tightened her grip on her bag and began walking.

The path led uphill, shaded by olive trees. The air was warm, but a soft breeze kept it comfortable. Daphne followed the winding road, her heart beating faster with each step.

She didn't know what she would find at the end of the path. She didn't know if anyone lived in the house. She didn't know what secrets her grandfather had left behind. But she kept walking, one step at a time, toward the truth.

The path grew narrower as Daphne climbed, the village slowly disappearing behind her. Olive trees lined the road, their silver-green leaves shimmering in the afternoon light. The air smelled of earth and wild herbs, and somewhere in the distance she could hear the faint clang of goat bells drifting across the hillside.

She paused to catch her breath, adjusting the strap of her bag. The velvet pouch inside felt heavier with every step, as if the cylinder were absorbing the weight of everything she didn't yet understand. She wiped her forehead and continued walking.

The road curved gently to the left, revealing a stretch of low stone walls and terraced fields. The landscape was quiet, almost unnervingly so. No cars. No voices. Only the rustle of leaves and the rhythmic crunch of gravel beneath her shoes.

She checked the map again. According to her grandfather's notes, the house should be somewhere beyond the next bend. She folded the paper carefully and slipped it back into her pocket.

Her pulse quickened.

The path leveled out, and the trees thinned. Ahead, perched on a gentle rise, stood a house.

Her breath caught.

It was older than she expected — a two-story stone structure with faded blue shutters and a tiled roof weathered by decades of sun and wind. A fig tree grew beside the porch, its branches heavy with fruit. The yard was enclosed by a low stone wall, and a narrow gate hung slightly askew.

Daphne stopped several yards away, her heart pounding. She felt as if she had stepped into one of her grandfather's stories — the ones he used to tell her when she was a child, about summers on the island, about the sea, about a house filled with books and secrets.

But he had never mentioned this house. Not once.

She approached slowly, her footsteps soft on the dirt path. The house looked lived-in — not pristine, but cared for. A clay pot filled with basil sat on the porch. A pair of sandals rested near the door.

Someone was home.

Daphne hesitated. She took a step back, her pulse racing. She didn't know what to do. She didn't know what to say. She didn't know how to explain why she was here.

She reached for her phone, her hands trembling slightly. She typed a message to Tasos.

I'm here. At the house. Someone lives in it.

She hesitated, then added:

I don't know what to do.

She hit send and lowered the phone, staring at the house as if it might speak to her.

A soft breeze rustled the fig leaves. A bird landed on the stone wall, tilting its head as if studying her. The world felt suspended, waiting.

Daphne reached out and held on to the low stone fence, steadying herself as she looked up at the old house. The stones were warm from the sun, rough beneath her palm — and then suddenly, horribly, *not* rough. Her fingers sank into something soft and damp.

She jerked her hand back instantly.

A small, strangled sound escaped her — half-gasp, half-whimper — far louder than she meant it to be. She froze, mortified, certain that whoever lived inside the house must have heard her.

But the embarrassment lasted only a heartbeat.

Because now her mind had seized on something far more urgent.

What was that? Her pulse spiked. *Was it alive? Was it mold? Some kind of fungus? Oh God — was it animal droppings? Did she just touch something full of bacteria? Parasites? Something that could infect her?*

The house, the mystery, the possibility of someone watching her — all of it vanished from her thoughts. Her entire world narrowed to her hand, her skin, the unknown substance clinging to her.

She dropped her bag to the ground and frantically dug through it, tossing aside her notebook, her water bottle, her sunglasses case. Her hands shook as she searched.

"Where are they, where are they, where are they—"

Finally, her fingers closed around the familiar plastic packet. She ripped it open with the desperation of someone defusing a bomb and scrubbed her hands with a disinfecting wipe so aggressively her skin turned pink. She wiped every finger, every nail, every crease of her palm. Then she used a second wipe. And a third. Only when her hands were clean — *truly* clean — did she let out a shaky breath.

She glanced back at the house. If anyone had seen her, well… that was a problem for later. Right now, the only thing that mattered was that she was not — as far as she could tell — dying of some obscure fence-related infection. She stuffed the wipes back into the packet, took another steadying breath, and tried to remember why she had come here in the first place.

Her phone buzzed.

Stay calm. Don't knock yet. I'm calling you.

A moment later, her phone rang. She answered immediately.

"Daphne," Tasos said, his voice steady. "Tell me what you see."

She swallowed. "It's… it's beautiful. Old. Someone's living here. There are shoes on the porch. Plants."

"Okay," he said. "That means you shouldn't approach the door yet. You don't know who's inside."

"I know," she whispered. "But this is the house. I'm sure of it."

"I believe you," he said. "But you need to take this slowly."

She closed her eyes, trying to steady her breathing. "What do I do?"

"For now," he said, "walk around the property. Don't go inside. Don't knock. Just look. Get a sense of the place."

She nodded, even though he couldn't see her. "Okay."

"And Daphne?"

"Yes?"

"Keep your phone on. I'll stay with you."

His voice grounded her. She took a slow breath and began walking along the stone wall, keeping a respectful distance from the house. The yard was simple — a few potted plants, a wooden bench, a small shed tucked behind the fig tree. Everything looked lived-in, but nothing looked new. Whoever lived here had been here a long time.

She reached the side of the house and stopped. A narrow window was cracked open, and she could hear faint movement inside — footsteps, maybe, or the soft clatter of dishes. She stepped back quickly, her heart racing.

"Someone's definitely home," she whispered into the phone.

"Then don't get too close," Tasos said, "if you're not ready to talk to them yet."

She continued around the back of the house. The land sloped gently downward, revealing a view of the sea in the distance — a shimmering expanse of blue stretching toward the horizon. The sight stole her breath.

Her grandfather had stood here. He had looked at this same view. He had written about this place with love and longing.

She felt a sudden ache in her chest.

"Are you okay?" Tasos asked.

"Yes," she said softly. "I just… I can see the sea."

She walked a little farther, stopping near a cluster of wildflowers growing along the edge of the property. The petals swayed gently in the breeze, their colors bright against the stone wall.

She crouched down, touching one of the flowers lightly. "It's peaceful here," she murmured.

"It is," Tasos said. "Lefkada has a way of slowing everything down."

She stood and looked back at the house. The shutters were closed on the upper floor, but the lower windows were open, letting in the afternoon air. She wondered who lived there. She wondered what they knew. She wondered if they had ever met her grandfather.

She wondered if they were expecting her.

"Daphne," Tasos said gently, "you should head back to the village soon. You've seen enough for today."

She hesitated. "I feel like I'm supposed to do something."

"You did," he said. "You found the house."

She nodded slowly. "Right."

She took one last look at the house — the faded shutters, the fig tree, the quiet porch — and turned away. She walked back down the path, her steps slow but steady.

When she reached the village, she returned to the same small café she had visited in the morning and sat at an outdoor table. She ordered a glass of water and unfolded the map, studying it carefully as she traced the route she had taken.

The café owner, a man in his late fifties with a gentle face and a towel slung over his shoulder, stepped outside when he noticed her lingering over the map. "Καλημέρα!" he greeted her warmly. He continued in English, noticing the map on her table and assuming she was a tourist. Daphne ordered a Greek coffee and a peynirli — the boat-shaped bread filled with cheese that Tasos had recommended.

When the man returned with her order, she looked up at him and said, in a serious tone, "May I ask you something?" The owner pulled out the chair across from her, as if sensing she needed more than directions. "Of course," he said. Daphne tapped the map lightly. "Do you know who lives in the old stone house up on the hill?" The man's eyes softened with recognition. "Ah. That house. Yes, a woman lives there. Evanthia. And her son, Yannis. They've been there many years."

Daphne felt her pulse quicken. "You know them?" The owner nodded, leaning back in his chair. "Since she was a little girl. Quiet child. Kind. Keeps to herself now. Life hasn't been simple for her." He didn't elaborate, but the weight in his voice made Daphne's chest tighten. She thanked him, and he patted her hand gently before standing. "Welcome to the island."

She finished her coffee and her peynirli, then gathered her things to head back to the guesthouse. It was still early, but she wasn't ready to return to the old house. She needed time to think, time to prepare. She walked slowly through the village, trying to take in the landscape and the quiet charm of the place, but her thoughts wouldn't let her. All she could focus on was tomorrow — the moment she would stand in front of the house and meet whoever lived there now.

Back at the guesthouse, she took a shower and went out onto the balcony. The sky was beginning to shift toward evening, the light turning soft and amber. Her mind churned with possibilities, rehearsing what she might say to the woman the next day when she finally approached the house her grandfather had sent her to find. The thought unsettled her, and she had to take several deep breaths to steady herself. She needed to sleep well. She needed her energy for tomorrow — energy and courage.

She lay down earlier than she normally would, hoping exhaustion might finally catch up with her. But even as the room darkened and the village settled into its quiet evening rhythm, her mind refused to slow. Every time she closed her eyes, she pictured the house, the doorway, the woman she would have to speak to. She kept rehearsing the same simple sentences, trying to make them sound natural in her head, trying to imagine how the conversation might begin. The more she practiced, the more restless she felt.

Eventually she turned off the lamp and forced herself to breathe evenly, reminding herself that she had done everything she could for now. Tomorrow would come whether she was ready or not. She needed rest, not more rehearsing. She pulled the sheet over her shoulder, shifted once, then again, and finally let her body sink into the mattress. With the balcony door slightly open and the faint sound of cicadas drifting in, she closed her eyes and willed herself to sleep.

CHAPTER 10

Daphne woke earlier than she expected, the pale morning light slipping through the curtains and easing her into the day ahead. For a moment she stayed still, listening to the soft hum of the village as it slowly came to life, and the reminder of what awaited her settled over her with quiet insistence. She swung her legs out of bed and stood, stretching the stiffness from her shoulders, the cool floor steady beneath her feet. Drawn by the faint brightness outside, she stepped onto the balcony and let the morning air wash over her. The sky was a gentle blue, brushed with the first strokes of gold. Below, the village was waking slowly — a shopkeeper rolling up a metal shutter, a cat padding along a sun-warmed wall, the distant clatter of dishes from someone's open kitchen window.

Daphne leaned on the railing and breathed deeply. She needed to gather her thoughts, to shape the words she would use when she returned to the old house. She needed to be ready.

But every time she tried to form the words, they scattered.

Hello, my name is Daphne Stavrides…
No, too formal.

My grandfather lived in your house…
Too abrupt.

I think you might know something about my grandfather…
Too vague.

She sighed, pressing her fingers to her temples.

Who was this woman? The café owner had spoken of her with familiarity, even affection. He had known her since she was a little girl. That meant she wasn't a recent tenant. She wasn't a stranger who had simply moved into the old stone house. She belonged here. She had roots on this island. But what kind of roots?

Daphne tried to imagine possibilities. Maybe the woman was a distant relative — a distant niece of her grandfather's, or the granddaughter of one of his cousins. She could even be connected through an old marriage in the family, some distant in-law whose name had faded over the years. Or perhaps she was the widow of a cousin or nephew, someone who had remained tied to the family long after others had drifted away. Or maybe the woman had no connection to her grandfather at all. Maybe she was simply someone who had lived there for years, someone who might remember him only vaguely, if at all.

Or maybe — and this possibility made her pulse quicken — maybe the woman knew him well. Maybe she had known him better than anyone.

Daphne closed her eyes, steadying herself. She couldn't let her imagination run wild. She needed to stay grounded, calm, open. She needed to ask questions carefully, respectfully. She needed to listen.

She stayed on the balcony until the sun rose fully, warming the hillside. When she finally stepped back inside, she felt a little steadier. She showered, dressed, and tied her hair back. She checked the velvet pouch in her bag. She didn't take out the cylinder. She didn't need to. Just knowing it was there was enough.

Downstairs, the guesthouse owner greeted her with a warm smile and a plate of fresh bread, cheese, and olives.

"Καλημέρα," she said. Good morning.

"Καλημέρα," Daphne replied, grateful for the kindness.

She ate slowly, letting the simple meal ground her. The bread was warm, the cheese soft and tangy, the olives briny and rich. It reminded her of the meals her grandfather used to make — rustic, unfussy, comforting. She wondered if he had learned to cook like that here, in this village, in this house. When she finished, she thanked the woman and stepped outside.

The village was beginning to stir. A few people swept their doorsteps, a man carried crates of fruit to the small market, and a group of children chased each other near the square. The air buzzed with quiet energy. Daphne walked through the village slowly, letting herself absorb the details — the chipped paint on the shutters, the scent of basil growing in pots, the sound of someone humming as they hung laundry. She needed this grounding. She needed to feel connected to the place before she approached the house again.

She wandered for nearly an hour, circling the square, walking down narrow lanes, pausing to watch a fisherman mend his nets near the small harbor. The sea shimmered in the distance, calm and inviting. The island felt both familiar and foreign, like a place she had known in another life.

She wondered whether it was too early to go to the house and knock on the door. Would the occupants even be awake at this hour. She decided to wander a little longer, letting the village settle into its morning before she made her way there.

By eleven o'clock, the sun was high and warm. Daphne returned to the guesthouse briefly to refill her water bottle, then stepped back outside.

It was time.

She followed the narrow road out of the square, her steps slower now, more deliberate. The olive trees rustled softly in the breeze, their silver-green leaves shimmering in the light. The path curved gently upward, and soon the house came into view — weathered stone walls, faded blue shutters, a fig tree leaning protectively over the porch.

She stopped at the gate, her heart pounding.

She wiped her palms on her jeans, took a breath, and pushed the gate open.

The hinges creaked.

She walked up the short path to the porch and knocked.

The sound echoed through the house — one knock, then another. She waited, her pulse thudding in her ears.

Footsteps approached.

The door opened.

A woman stood in the doorway — tall, with dark hair streaked with silver and eyes that held a guarded intelligence. She looked to be in her late fifties or early sixties. She wore a simple linen dress and held a dish towel in one hand.

For a moment, neither of them spoke. Then the woman's expression shifted — not recognition, but something close to it. A flicker of surprise, quickly masked.

"Καλημέρα," the woman said. Good morning.

"Καλημέρα," Daphne replied, her voice steady despite the tightness in her chest. "My name is Daphne," she said in English, too nervous to speak Greek at that moment.

The woman studied her face with unsettling intensity. "You were here yesterday," she said in English but with a strong Greek accent.

Daphne swallowed. "Yes. I… I wasn't sure if anyone lived here."

The woman's eyes narrowed slightly. "People live here."

"I can see that now," Daphne said softly, feeling embarrassed. "I'm sorry if I startled you."

The woman didn't respond immediately. She glanced at Daphne's face again, as if searching for something she couldn't quite place.

"What do you want?" she asked, not unkindly, but with a firmness that suggested she didn't entertain strangers lightly.

Daphne took a breath. "My name is Daphne Stavrides. I'm looking for information about someone who lived in this house a long time ago."

The woman's grip tightened on the dish towel. "Who?"

"My grandfather," Daphne said. "His name was Yiannis Papadakis."

The woman inhaled sharply — a small, involuntary sound. Her gaze flicked over Daphne's face, lingering on her eyes. She stepped back slightly, as if bracing herself.

Before she could respond, a young man's voice came from inside.

"Μαμά; Ποιος είναι;" Mom? Who is it?

A young man appeared behind her — tall, broad-shouldered, with dark hair and the same sharp eyes. He looked to be in his mid-twenties. When he saw Daphne, he stopped abruptly, confusion crossing his face.

The woman turned to him but didn't say anything.

He insisted, "Who is she?"

Daphne felt her throat tighten. "I'm sorry to intrude," she said. "I just… I'm trying to understand my grandfather's past. He left me a letter. It led me here."

The young man's expression softened slightly, curiosity flickering in his eyes.

The woman looked at Daphne again, her face unreadable.

"What did you say your name was?" she asked quietly.

"Daphne," she said. "Daphne Stavrides. My mother is Maria Papadakis."

The woman closed her eyes briefly, as if steadying herself. When she opened them again, they were softer, but still wary.

"You should come in," she said.

Daphne hesitated. "Are you sure?"

"Yes," the woman said. "If you've come this far, you should come in."

She stepped aside, and Daphne crossed the threshold.

The interior of the house was warm and lived-in. The walls were lined with shelves filled with books, framed photographs, and small objects that looked handmade. A woven rug covered the floor. The air smelled faintly of onion.

The young man stood near the table, watching her with a mixture of curiosity and caution.

The woman gestured toward a chair. "Sit."

Daphne sat, her hands clasped tightly in her lap.

The woman remained standing. "I'm Evanthia Papadaki," she said. "And this is my son, Yannis."

Daphne's breath caught. "Papadaki," she repeated softly.

Evanthia nodded once.

"That's… my mother's maiden name," Daphne said. "My grandfather's name."

"I know," Evanthia replied quietly.

Daphne looked at her, confused. "How?"

Evanthia didn't answer immediately. Instead, she walked to a small wooden coffee table near the sofa. She picked up a framed photograph and held it for a moment before handing it to Daphne.

Daphne took it carefully. The photo showed a little girl — no more than six — standing beside a man in his early thirties. The man was unmistakably her grandfather. Younger, leaner, but with the same gentle eyes and the same quiet confidence in his posture. His hand rested lightly on the girl's shoulder.

Daphne's breath caught. "This is you," she whispered.

Evanthia nodded.

"And him," Daphne said, her voice trembling. "My grandfather."

"Yes," Evanthia said softly. "He was my father."

The words hit Daphne like a physical blow.

She looked at the photograph again — the girl's shy smile, the man's protective stance, the unmistakable connection between them. Her grandfather had another daughter. A daughter he had never told anyone about. A daughter who had lived her entire life on this island. Daphne set the photograph down carefully, her hands shaking.

"I didn't know," she said. "None of us knew."

Evanthia's expression softened, but only slightly. "He kept many things to himself."

Yannis stepped closer, his voice quiet but steady. "Why did you come?"

Daphne reached into her bag and pulled out the letter. She set it gently on the table, placing it face-down and pointing to the small sketch of the island drawn at the bottom.

"He left this for me," she said. "He wanted me to come here."

Evanthia stared at the sketch, her face unreadable. "He always said someone would come one day."

Daphne swallowed. "He told you that?"

"Yes," Evanthia said. "But he didn't say who. Or when."

Yannis crossed his arms. "Why now?"

Daphne hesitated. She couldn't tell them everything — not yet. She didn't know them. She didn't know what they knew. She didn't know what her grandfather had told them.

"I'm trying to understand," she said carefully. "I'm trying to figure out what he wanted me to find."

Evanthia exchanged a glance with her son — a silent conversation Daphne couldn't interpret.

Then Evanthia said, "Come back tomorrow morning. We'll talk then. I need some time to gather all the things I need to show you."

Daphne stood slowly. "Thank you. I'll come back."

Evanthia walked her to the door. Before Daphne stepped outside, the woman spoke again — softer this time.

"You have his eyes," she said. "Just like Yannis."

Daphne felt her throat tighten. "I know." After a short pause, she added, "I miss him."

Evanthia's expression flickered — a brief, fragile crack in her composure. "We all do."

Daphne stepped out onto the porch. She walked down the path, her heart pounding, her mind racing. She had met them. She had stepped inside the house. She had seen the photograph. She had taken the first real step into her grandfather's hidden world.

CHAPTER 11

The walk back to the village felt heavier than the one that had brought her up the hill. Daphne moved slowly, her mind buzzing with too many thoughts to hold at once. The photograph, Evanthia's voice, the way Yannis had looked at her — curious, cautious — all of it swirled inside her like a storm she couldn't outrun.

Her grandfather had another daughter.

The words kept repeating, not as a sentence but as a sensation — a shift in gravity, a rearranging of the world she thought she knew. She tried to picture him as a young man, living in this house, raising a little girl. Hadn't her mother been born yet? Did her grandpa raise two girls living in separate homes? Who was this woman's mother? Daphne tried to imagine what had happened, why he had left, why he had never spoken of it. But every time she reached for an answer, it slipped away.

By the time she reached the village square, it was already late afternoon, the sun casting long, slanting shadows across the cobblestones. Daphne wasn't sure where the time had gone. Her visit to the house had been briefer than she'd expected, so she supposed she must have walked back too slowly, drifting through the paths with her mind elsewhere. Only now did she realize how deeply she'd been absorbed in her thoughts. And though the visit had been short, she had learned more than she could manage in a single day. In a way, she was grateful the woman had asked her to return tomorrow instead of pressing her with more questions now. She needed time — to breathe, to absorb, to steady herself before facing whatever came next.

On her way to the guesthouse, she noticed a few people lingering outside the *kafeneio*, sipping coffee and speaking in low voices. Their conversations drifted through the air like soft threads, but Daphne couldn't catch a single word. She walked straight to the guesthouse, climbed the stairs to her room, and closed the door behind her. The quiet hit her like a wave. She leaned against the door for a moment, letting the silence settle around her. Her heart was still beating too fast. Her hands were trembling. She felt as if she had stepped into a story she didn't know the beginning of — one she wasn't sure she had the right to finish.

She walked to the balcony and stepped outside. From here, she couldn't see the house, but she could feel it — a presence on the hill, waiting. She wrapped her arms around herself, trying to steady her breathing.

She had an aunt.

The thought felt unreal. She had grown up believing her mother was an only child, that her grandfather's life before America was a closed chapter. He had never spoken of siblings, cousins, or anyone else. He had never spoken of a daughter. Why?

She closed her eyes, trying to summon a memory — any memory — that might hint at this hidden life. But all she could see was the man she had known: gentle, quiet, steady. A man who had taught her how to tie knots, how to read the stars, how to savor the small rituals of their Greek-American home — the way he'd say *"σιγά-σιγά"* to remind her to take things slowly. A man who had always seemed to carry a sadness he never explained.

Maybe this was the sadness.

She stayed on the balcony until the sun started to set. The air was a little cooler now, touched by the scent of jasmine drifting from a nearby garden. The village lights flickered on one by one, casting a warm glow across the hillside. When she finally returned inside, she felt drained, as if the day had pulled something essential from her.

She changed into comfortable clothes, washed her face, and sat on the bed with her notebook. She opened it to a blank page and stared at it for a long moment before writing a single line:

Why didn't you tell us?

She waited for an answer to rise — a memory, a clue, something — but nothing came. She closed the notebook and set it aside.

Her phone buzzed. A message from Tasos.

Did you go to the house? Are you okay?

She hesitated before typing back.

Yes. I met them. It's… a lot. I'll explain tomorrow.

His reply came quickly.

I'm here if you need anything. Try to rest.

She appreciated the simplicity of it. No questions. No pressure. Just presence.

She placed her phone on the nightstand and lay down. The room was quiet except for the distant chirping of cicadas. She closed her eyes and kept replaying the moment Evanthia handed her the photograph — the weight of it, the truth of it, the way it had shifted everything she thought she knew.

Eventually, exhaustion pulled her under.

She woke early the next morning, the room still dim. For a moment she didn't remember where she was. Then the events of the previous day rushed back, and her stomach tightened.

She sat up slowly, rubbing her eyes. The air felt cool and fresh, carrying the faint scent of the sea. She stood, stretched, and walked to the balcony. The sky was pale blue, streaked with the first hints of sunrise. The village was quiet, still waking.

She needed to return to the house. She needed to hear the rest. She needed to understand. But she also needed to steady herself first.

She got ready and went downstairs. The guesthouse owner greeted her with a warm smile and pointed her toward the tiny dining area. "We have a lot of fresh fruit today, and we just made a big batch of yogurt."

Daphne obliged. She ate slowly, letting the simple meal steady her. The fruit was sweet, the yogurt creamy and rich. As the owner passed by, she paused. "Put some chopped walnuts and honey in your yogurt. It's a great combination, you'll see."

Daphne had eaten yogurt with walnuts and honey countless times in Astoria, but she didn't want to spoil the woman's enthusiasm. So she went to the small buffet, added the toppings as suggested, and then pretended to be pleasantly surprised by the taste. The owner beamed, clearly delighted.

When Daphne finished, she thanked the woman warmly and stepped outside. She set off toward the house again, following the same path she had taken the day before. Yet this time, it felt as though she reached it in half the time. Maybe she had walked faster without realizing it. The familiar landmarks appeared sooner than she expected, drawing her back toward the place that had unsettled her so deeply the day before. She knocked softly on the door.

She waited, her pulse thudding in her ears. Footsteps approached. The door opened. Evanthia stood in the doorway, her expression unreadable.

"You came," she said.

"Yes," Daphne replied. "I said I would."

Evanthia stepped aside. "Come in. We have much to discuss."

Daphne crossed the threshold, her pulse quickening. Yannis stood near the table, arms crossed, watching her with the same guarded curiosity as before. The photograph still sat on the coffee table, exactly where she had placed it. The room felt different today — not warmer, not colder, but charged with something new. Expectation. Tension. Possibility.

Evanthia gestured toward the chair. "Sit."

Daphne sat. Evanthia remained standing for a moment, studying her. Then she spoke.

"You deserve to know the truth," she said. "All of it."

Daphne's breath caught. She wasn't ready. But she was here. And she would listen.

Evanthia took a slow breath.

"It's time you learned who your grandfather really was."

CHAPTER 12

Evanthia moved toward the small kitchen alcove, her steps slow, deliberate. She reached for a kettle, filled it at the sink, and set it on the stove. The soft hiss of the flame filled the silence. She opened a cabinet, took down two mismatched mugs, and placed them on the counter with a quiet clink.

Daphne was sitting at the table, her pulse still unsteady from the walk up the hill. She wished she had taken a moment to catch her breath before coming in. Now this anxiety was making her heart beat so fast, she was unable to say a word. For a second she was afraid she might be having a heart attack. Then she reasoned with herself. It was the uphill walk and the anxiety; it was normal. She took in a deep breath, held it, then exhaled. Then a second deep breath with a long exhale, then a third. She started to feel calmer. Now, instead of her own heartbeat, she could hear the faint ticking of a clock somewhere in the next room, steady and patient.

Evanthia was taking her time and Daphne was thankful for it. She took a few more deep breaths and waited patiently, her hands clasped in her lap. She didn't want to rush Evanthia. Whatever this story was, it had lived inside her for decades. It deserved time.

When the kettle began to whistle softly, Evanthia poured the hot water over loose tea leaves, the steam rising in gentle curls. She carried the mugs to the table and set one in front of Daphne before finally sitting down across from her.

For a moment, she said nothing. She wrapped her hands around her mug, staring into the swirling tea as if it held the past she was about to unearth. Then she looked up.

"You should understand something before I begin," she said quietly. "My mother never wanted this story told. Not to anyone. Not even to me, when I was young. But I knew anyway. Children always know more than adults think."

Her voice was steady, but there was a tightness beneath it — a strain that suggested she had rehearsed these words many times in her mind, but never spoken them aloud.

Daphne nodded, encouraging her to continue.

Evanthia took a slow breath. "Your grandfather… Yiannis… he was a good man. A complicated man, but a good one. And he loved my mother. Truly loved her."

Daphne felt her chest tighten. She had expected this.

"They met when they were young," Evanthia continued. "Barely more than children, really. My mother was from a family that had lived on this side of the island for generations. In Nydri. Your grandfather's family… they were from the other side, from Kalamitsi. Close enough to visit, far enough to feel like strangers here."

She paused, her gaze drifting toward the window. "There was a feud between the families. Old, stupid, bitter. No one even remembers how it started. But it meant they were not supposed to be together."

Daphne leaned forward slightly. "But they were."

"Yes," Evanthia said. "They were."

She took another sip of tea, her hands trembling just slightly.

"They tried to keep it secret at first. Meeting in the olive groves, by the cliffs, anywhere they could be alone. But secrets don't stay hidden long on an island. People talk. And when the families found out…" She shook her head. "It was ugly. My mother's brothers threatened him. His family forbade him from seeing her. They said it would bring shame, ruin, disaster."

Daphne felt a flicker of anger on her grandfather's behalf — and on Evanthia's mother's.

"But they didn't stop," Evanthia said. "They loved each other too much. They thought they could outlast the feud. That people would calm down eventually. That love would be enough."

Her voice softened. "It wasn't."

The room felt smaller suddenly, the air thicker.

"When my mother became pregnant with me," Evanthia said, "everything changed. The feud became a weapon. People were starting to talk and say terrible things. My mother was called names. My father was accused of dishonoring her. Both families blamed the other. It was… unbearable."

Daphne swallowed hard. "I'm so sorry."

Evanthia gave a small, sad smile. "It was a long time ago. But thank you."

She looked down at her hands. "My father wanted to marry her, you know. He asked her many times. But she said no. She said she wouldn't drag him into the feud again. She said she wouldn't let him be torn apart by two families who hated each other."

"And so he left?" asked Daphne.

"Not right away. Not for a few years. Because in the meantime I was born, and he didn't want anyone to call me a bastard. So he gave me his name. He made sure my mother and I would be fine without him. He gave us this house. Quietly. Secretly. Only the three of us knew. He wanted us to be safe. To have a place that was ours."

"And then he left Lefkada forever," Daphne rushed to conclude.

"He left Lefkada forever, yes. My mother preferred that people looked at her with pity rather than with hate. She preferred they see her as a woman abandoned with a child, instead of someone who had fueled an old feud and didn't care about honor, family, or the rest of the island. It was easier that way."

She paused, her eyes distant.

Daphne felt a shiver run through her. "My mother never knew about this house or you or any ties that my grandpa still held here."

"No," Evanthia said. "She didn't."

The kettle clicked softly as it cooled on the stove.

"Those few years that I spent with him were the most wonderful years of my life," Evanthia continued. "He didn't live with us but he visited us often. He helped my mother with repairs. He brought me books, toys, little things he thought I would like. He was gentle. Patient. He taught me how to tie knots, how to read the stars, how to listen to the sea."

Daphne's breath caught. "He taught me those things too."

A flicker of something — pain, longing, recognition — crossed Evanthia's face. "I'm not surprised."

She looked down again, her voice quieter now. "But then… things changed."

Daphne waited, her heart pounding. She expected to hear how her grandfather left everything behind.

"He met your grandmother," Evanthia said.

The words landed like a stone.

"He didn't mean for it to happen," she added quickly. "He wasn't looking for someone else. But life… life doesn't always follow the paths we expect. Your grandmother was kind. Smart. Steady. She came from a good family. A respected family. And she loved him. And of course there was the pressure for him to marry. From his family. The longer he stayed unmarried the more they suspected that my mother was still in his life."

Daphne felt a strange mix of emotions — confusion, guilt, disappointment.

"So he didn't marry my grandmother for love?" she asked. "He married her to prove something to his family and to the rest of the…"

"Oh, no, that's not what I'm saying," interrupted Evanthia. "He loved her very much." She paused for a few seconds. "And my mother knew. He told her he planned to leave for America with her. He spoke about her with sweetness, with... love. So my mother told him... she told him to leave."

"She sent him away," Daphne whispered.

"Yes," Evanthia said. "She said she could never rebuild her life while he was here. That it was selfish of him to have two women who loved him, and for her to have no husband. She said he deserved a chance at a normal life. A life without lies. Without shame. Without the feud."

Daphne felt tears prick her eyes. "That must have been so hard for her."

"It was," Evanthia said. "But she was strong. Stronger than anyone gave her credit for."

"And then...he married my grandmother, and together they left for New York," Daphne said softly.

"He married her after he left. But it doesn't matter. He married her and they had a daughter, your mother. And he built a new life."

Daphne felt a knot tighten in her chest. "Did he ever... forget you?"

"No," Evanthia said firmly. "Never. He wrote to us. He sent money often. He asked for photographs. He wanted to come back many times to see me, but my mother told him not to. She said it would only make things harder."

"And you?" Daphne asked. "How did you feel?"

Evanthia hesitated. "I was a child," she said finally. "And children… children don't understand sacrifice. They only understand absence."

She looked directly at Daphne now, her eyes shining with something raw and unguarded.

"I knew he was my father. I knew he loved me. But I also knew he had another family. A family he lived with. A family he chose."

Daphne's breath caught.

"I was jealous," Evanthia said simply. "Of your mother. Of you. Of the life you had with him. I tried not to be. I tried to be grateful for what I had. But it hurt. It hurt every day."

Daphne felt tears spill down her cheeks. She didn't wipe them away.

"My mother told me not to blame him," Evanthia said. "She said he was doing what he had to do. She said he was trying to protect us. But I was a child. And children… children want their fathers."

The room was silent except for the faint ticking of the clock.

Daphne swallowed hard. "I didn't know," she whispered. "I didn't know any of this."

"I know," Evanthia said gently. "Your mother didn't know either. He kept the two worlds separate. He thought it was kinder that way."

Daphne shook her head slowly. "He must have felt so guilty."

"He did," Evanthia said. "All his life."

She looked straight into Daphne's eyes. "And now… now you're here. And I don't know what that means yet. For you. For me. For any of us."

Daphne took a shaky breath. "I don't either."

Evanthia nodded, her expression softening. "But we will figure it out."

The sunlight shifted across the floor, warm and bright. For the first time since entering the house, Daphne felt the weight of the truth settle into place — heavy, painful, but real.

Her grandfather had lived two lives. Two loves. Two families. And she was sitting across from the woman who had lived in the shadow of that truth her entire life.

CHAPTER 13

For a moment, no one spoke. Sunlight slanted across the table, on the forgotten mugs of tea. Daphne felt the silence settle around them — not empty, but full, dense with the gravity of a truth that had finally been spoken aloud.

Evanthia sat very still, her hands folded neatly in front of her, her gaze lowered. When she looked up again, she saw Yannis standing near the doorway of his room.

"How long have you been standing there?" she asked.

 "Not long," Yannis said. But I could hear everything from my room anyway. I wanted to come say hello but I didn't want to interrupt."

"Come. This concerns you too. You know most of it anyway but I'd like you to be here."

Yannis came closer to the table and looked at Daphne.

"I guess we're related," he said, smiling.

Daphne realized how much his smile was like her grandfather's and she couldn't help but smile too. "We are related," she repeated.

Then Evanthia pushed her chair back gently and stood.

"There is more you should know," she said. "But it's easier to show you than to sit here and talk about it."

She moved toward the far side of the room — not down a hallway, not into some new, unmentioned space, but simply toward a door Daphne hadn't noticed before, half-hidden behind a tall wooden cabinet. The door was old, its paint chipped, its brass handle worn smooth by years of use.

Evanthia opened it slowly.

"This leads to my mother's room," she said. "I haven't changed much since she passed. It's where I keep the things he sent. The things she saved."

Daphne stood, her legs unsteady but willing. Yannis stepped aside to let her pass, offering a small, reassuring nod. She followed Evanthia through the doorway into a small, sunlit room that felt suspended in time.

The air was cooler here, touched with the faint scent of lavender and old paper. A narrow bed sat against the wall, covered with a faded quilt. A wooden desk stood beneath the window, its surface neatly arranged with small objects — a ceramic bowl, a stack of folded linens, a few framed photographs turned face-down.

Evanthia crossed to the desk and carefully opened a drawer.

"My mother kept everything," she said. "Even when she pretended she didn't care. Even when she told him not to write anymore."

She lifted out a small wooden box, worn smooth at the corners, and set it gently on the desk.

"He sent letters," she said. "Many in the beginning. Then less and less. But he never stopped sending them."

Daphne felt her breath catch. She stepped closer, drawn to the box as if it held a piece of her grandfather's voice.

Evanthia opened the lid.

Inside were envelopes — some yellowed with age, others still crisp, their edges sharp. Daphne could see her grandfather's handwriting on the topmost one, the familiar slant of his letters.

"He wrote about his life in America," Evanthia said. "About the work he found. About the winters he hated. About the food he missed. He wrote about your mother. About you."

Daphne swallowed hard. "He never said anything about you."

"He didn't want to burden you," Evanthia said. "He believed the past was his to carry."

She closed the box gently and placed her hand on top of it, as if steadying herself.

"When my mother died," she continued, "I wrote to him. I told him she was gone. I told him he didn't need to carry the guilt anymore. Because I knew that, even though he had built a new life and was happy, he still felt guilty for leaving us."

Daphne looked up sharply. "Did he write back?"

"Yes," Evanthia said. "A short letter. Just a few lines. He said he was sorry. He said he wished he had been braver. He said he hoped I would forgive him one day."

Her voice tightened. "I didn't write back."

Daphne felt a twist of pain. "Why not?"

"Because I didn't know how," Evanthia said simply. "Grief makes everything sharp. And I didn't want to reopen the wound."

Evanthia got up and walked to a small cabinet in the corner. She opened it and took out a larger wooden box with a metal clasp.

"My mother kept this for him," she said. "She always believed he would come back one day."

She placed the box on the bed.

"She never opened it," Evanthia said. "She said it wasn't hers to open."

She looked at Daphne. "But I really think she didn't open it because it would be too painful. I opened it a couple of times. It filled in some blanks. I think you should read it too. It will help you understand."

Daphne hesitated, then sat on the edge of the bed and opened the clasp. Inside was a folded handkerchief embroidered with delicate blue thread. Beneath it lay a small leather-bound notebook.

Daphne lifted it gently.

Her grandfather's handwriting filled the first page.

"For the parts of my life I could not carry with me."

Her breath hitched.

Evanthia stepped closer. "It's his journal. Or part of it."

Daphne closed the notebook, overwhelmed. "I can only understand a few words here and there."

"It's OK," Yannis said. "I'll translate. If I can decipher that handwriting, that is."

"You don't have to look at it now," Evanthia said to Daphne. "Take your time. When you're ready, Yannis will help you."

Daphne placed the notebook back in the box and closed the lid.

When she looked up, Evanthia's expression had softened — no longer guarded, no longer distant, but open in a way that felt fragile and new.

"You and I..." Evanthia began, then paused. "We come from the same man. We carry different pieces of him. But they're pieces of the same whole."

Daphne felt her throat tighten. "I want to know you," she said. "Both of you."

Yannis stepped forward, his voice quiet. "We want to know you too."

The three of them stood there for a moment, the sunlight warm on their faces, the past settling gently between them. It wasn't forgiveness. It wasn't family love. Not yet. But it was the beginning of something that might one day become it.

Evanthia exhaled slowly. "Come," she said. "Let's go back to the kitchen. We should eat something. Stories like this... they take strength."

Daphne nodded, wiping her eyes. "Yes. I'd like that."

At that moment, Daphne felt she wasn't just uncovering her grandfather's past. She was stepping into her own future.

CHAPTER 14

Back in the kitchen, the sunlight had shifted across the floor, settling in a bright patch that warmed the tiles near the table. The mugs of tea sat where they had left them, the steam long gone, the surface of the liquid still and dark.

Evanthia moved quietly, almost automatically, opening a cupboard and taking out a plate of *koulourakia* she had baked the day before. She set them on the table without ceremony, as though offering food were the most natural way to steady the ground beneath their feet.

"Sit," she said gently.

Daphne did. Her legs felt heavy, as if the truth she had absorbed had settled into her bones. Yannis pulled out a chair across from her, but he didn't sit right away. He hovered for a moment, studying her with a kind of cautious empathy, then finally lowered himself into the seat. Evanthia remained standing for a moment longer, her hands braced on the back of her chair. She looked at Daphne with an expression that was both tender and searching.

"You've heard a lot today," she said. "More than anyone should have to hear in one morning."

Daphne nodded. "I needed to hear it."

"Yes," Evanthia said softly. "You did."

She sat down, folding her hands in her lap. For a moment, the three of them simply breathed in the same space, letting the quiet settle around them like a soft blanket. Then Evanthia spoke again.

"There's something else I want to tell you," she said. "Something about why he left for America. Not just the feud. Not just my mother's insistence. There was… another reason."

Daphne felt her pulse quicken. "What reason?"

Evanthia hesitated, her gaze drifting toward the window. Outside, the olive trees swayed gently in the breeze, their leaves shimmering silver in the sunlight.

"He was ashamed," she said finally. "Not of us. Never of us. But of himself."

Daphne frowned. "Ashamed?"

"Yes," Evanthia said. "He believed he had failed everyone. He believed he had ruined two families. He believed he had broken my mother's life, and that he would break your grandmother's too if he stayed."

Daphne felt a sharp ache in her chest. "He didn't break my grandmother's life."

"No," Evanthia agreed. "But he didn't know that then. He only saw the damage he had already caused. And he thought leaving was the only way to stop causing more."

She paused, her voice softening. "He didn't go to America for opportunity. He went because he thought he didn't deserve to stay."

Daphne closed her eyes, letting the words sink in. She had always imagined her grandfather as a man who left Greece because he wanted something bigger, something new. She had never imagined him as a man running from himself.

"When he arrived in the United States," Evanthia continued, "he wrote to my mother. He said he felt like a ghost. Like he had left pieces of himself scattered across the island, and he didn't know how to gather them again."

Daphne opened her eyes. "Did he ever find peace?"

Evanthia shook her head slowly. "I don't think so. Not fully. He built a life. He loved your grandmother and your mother. And of course he adored you. But the guilt… it stayed with him. It shaped him."

Daphne felt tears prick her eyes. "I wish he had told me."

"I know," Evanthia said. "But he wanted to protect you from the parts of his life he couldn't fix."

Yannis leaned forward slightly. "He wasn't a bad man," he said. "He was a man who made choices he didn't know how to live with."

Daphne nodded, wiping her eyes. "I know."

Evanthia reached across the table and placed her hand gently over Daphne's. "You don't have to carry his guilt," she said. "It was his. Not yours."

Daphne swallowed hard. "But I feel like I've inherited it."

"That's because you loved him," Evanthia said. "And because you're trying to understand him. But understanding doesn't mean carrying."

The words settled over Daphne like a soft, steadying weight.

For a moment, none of them spoke.

Then Yannis stood abruptly. "I'll get more tea," he said, moving toward the stove.

Evanthia watched him with a small smile. "He's always like this," she said. "When things get heavy, he tries to fix it with food or tea."

"It's a good instinct," Daphne said.

"It is," Evanthia agreed.

Yannis returned with a fresh pot of tea and poured it into their mugs. Its warm scent filled the room, soothing and familiar.

Daphne wrapped her hands around her mug, letting the heat seep into her palms.

"Can I ask you something?" she said quietly.

"Of course," Evanthia replied.

"Did he ever… talk about coming back? Really coming back?"

Evanthia nodded. "Many times. Especially after your grandmother died. He wrote that he felt untethered. That he wanted to see the island again. That he wanted to see me. And Yannis."

Daphne looked at Yannis, who lowered his gaze.

"But he didn't," Daphne said.

"No," Evanthia said. "He didn't."

"Why?"

Evanthia took a slow breath. "Because he was afraid. Afraid of reopening old wounds. Afraid of hurting your mother. Afraid of facing the past he had buried. So he kept postponing it."

Daphne felt her throat tighten. "He shouldn't have been afraid."

"No," Evanthia said gently. "But fear doesn't listen to reason."

Daphne stared into her tea, her thoughts swirling. "I wish I could talk to him now. I wish I could ask him why he didn't trust us with the truth."

Evanthia reached out again, her touch warm and steady. "He trusted you with the parts he thought you needed. He didn't trust himself with the rest."

Daphne nodded slowly, understanding in a way she hadn't before.

Yannis sat down again, his expression thoughtful. "You know," he said, "my mother always told me that people are shaped by the things they don't say as much as by the things they do."

Evanthia smiled faintly. "Your grandmother used to say that too."

Daphne looked between them — mother and son, two people who had lived with the consequences of her grandfather's silence for decades.

"I want to know everything," she said. "Not just the parts he wrote down. Not just the parts he hid. I want to know the whole story."

"You will," Evanthia said. "Through his journal. Through the stories. Through the people who remember him."

Daphne looked up. "Will you tell me more?"

"Yes," Evanthia said. "But first… you should rest. You've taken in enough for one day."

Daphne opened her mouth to protest, but Evanthia shook her head gently.

"Just take a little nap. We all do around this time." Then shaded slowly, reassuringly, "The past isn't going anywhere."

Daphne nodded, feeling the exhaustion settle into her limbs. "All right."

Yannis stood. "I'll show you the guest room."

Daphne followed him down the short hallway and stepped into a very small, simple room with a narrow bed and a window overlooking the olive trees.

"You can stay as long as you need," Yannis said.

Daphne nodded, her voice soft. "Thank you."

When he left, she sat on the edge of the bed and looked out the window. The trees swayed gently, their leaves whispering secrets she was only beginning to understand. She felt comfortable in this house with Evanthia and her son. And for the first time since arriving on the island, she didn't feel lost. She felt found. She was in a guest room, but she felt at home.

CHAPTER 15

Daphne didn't remember falling asleep. One moment she was staring at the olive trees outside the window, their branches swaying like slow-moving waves, and the next she was waking to the soft sound of footsteps in the hallway. For a moment she didn't move. The room was dimmer now, the afternoon light fading into the warm gold of early evening. The air smelled faintly of thyme and something sweet — maybe the *koulourakia* Evanthia had set out earlier. She sat up slowly, her body heavy with the kind of exhaustion that came not from physical effort but from emotional unraveling. Her mind felt full, stretched, as if every thought had to find a new place to settle.

There was a gentle knock on the door.

"Daphne?" Evanthia's voice was soft, careful. "Are you awake?"

"Yes," Daphne said, her voice rough from sleep.

The door opened a few inches, and Evanthia peeked inside. "I didn't want to wake you. You've been resting for a few hours."

Daphne blinked. "Hours?"

Evanthia nodded. "It's almost evening."

Daphne rubbed her eyes. "I didn't mean to sleep so long."

"You needed it," Evanthia said simply. "Come. There's something I want to show you before it gets dark."

Daphne stood, smoothing her hair with her fingers. She followed Evanthia down the short hallway and back into the main room. The kitchen was tidier now — the mugs washed, the table wiped clean. Yannis was sitting by the window, carving something small from a piece of olive wood. He looked up when Daphne entered and gave her a quiet nod.

"Feeling better?" he asked.

"A little," Daphne said.

He smiled faintly. "Good."

Evanthia gestured toward the door that led outside. "Come. It's just a short walk."

Daphne slipped on her shoes and followed her out into the warm evening air. The sky was streaked with pink and orange, the sun dipping low behind the hills. The cicadas had quieted, replaced by the soft chirping of crickets.

They walked along a narrow path behind the house, the earth dry beneath their feet. Olive trees lined the way, their branches arching overhead like a canopy. The air smelled of dust and wild herbs.

After a few minutes, they reached a small clearing. In the center stood a stone bench, worn smooth by time. Beyond it, the land sloped gently downward, offering a view of the sea in the distance — a thin line of shimmering silver.

"This was his place," Evanthia said quietly. "Your grandfather's."

Daphne looked around. The clearing felt peaceful, almost sacred. "He came here often?"

"Yes," Evanthia said. "When he needed to think. When he needed to breathe. When he needed to be alone."

Daphne walked to the bench and ran her fingers along the cool stone. "Did he come here with your mother?"

"Sometimes," Evanthia said. "But mostly he came alone. He said the sea helped him make sense of things."

Daphne sat down slowly. The stone was cool beneath her, grounding. Evanthia sat beside her, leaving a respectful space between them.

"He brought me here once," Evanthia said. "I was maybe six or seven. He told me that the sea doesn't judge. That it holds everything — the good, the bad, the things we wish we could forget."

Daphne felt a lump rise in her throat. "I wish he had brought me here."

"I'm sure he would have, if he could" Evanthia said gently.

They sat in silence for a moment, watching the sky shift colors.

"Before he left for America," Evanthia finally said, "he made a promise to my mother. A promise he also made to himself."

Daphne waited.

"He promised he would build a life he could be proud of," Evanthia said. "A life that would honor both families. A life that would make the pain worth something."

Daphne frowned. "I don't understand."

Evanthia looked out at the sea. "He believed that if he could build a good life in America — if he could be a good husband, a good father, a good man — then maybe the mistakes he made here wouldn't define him."

Daphne felt her chest tighten. "He tried."

"Yes," Evanthia said. "He tried very hard."

"But he still carried the guilt," added Daphne.

"He did," Evanthia said. "But he also carried hope. Hope that one day, the two parts of his life would not be enemies. Hope that one day, someone — maybe you — would understand him."

Daphne felt tears prick her eyes. "I'm trying."

"I know," Evanthia said softly. "And that's enough."

They sat in silence again, the sky darkening around them. The first stars began to appear, faint and trembling.

After a while, Evanthia stood. "There's something else I want to show you. It's not far."

Daphne followed her along a narrow path that wound between the olive trees. The air grew cooler as the sun dipped below the horizon. They walked until they reached a small stone wall, half-covered in vines.

Evanthia stopped.

"This," she said, "is where he told my mother goodbye."

Daphne felt her breath catch.

"He stood right here," Evanthia said, touching the wall. "He told her he would leave the island the next morning. He told her he would always carry her and me in his heart. And she told him to go and never look back."

Daphne closed her eyes, imagining the scene — the pain, the courage, the impossible choice.

"She cried," Evanthia said. "But she didn't let him see. She waited until he walked away."

Daphne opened her eyes. "Did he look back?"

Evanthia nodded. "Once. Just once."

Daphne felt tears spill down her cheeks.

"He carried that moment with him," Evanthia said. "All the way to America. All the way through his life."

Daphne took a shaky breath. "Thank you for bringing me here."

Evanthia placed a hand on her shoulder. "Come. It's getting dark."

They walked back to the house in silence, the stars brightening overhead. When they reached the door, Yannis was waiting for them, a lantern in his hand.

"Dinner's ready," he said.

Daphne smiled faintly. "Thank you."

They ate together at the small kitchen table — simple food, warm and comforting. Daphne felt the heaviness in her chest ease, replaced by something quieter, steadier.

When the meal was finished, Evanthia stood and began clearing the dishes. Daphne rose to help, but Evanthia shook her head.

"Sit," she said. "This will only take me a minute."

Daphne sat.

Yannis leaned back in his chair, studying her. "You're staying the night, right?"

Daphne hesitated. "If it's not too much trouble."

"It's not," Evanthia said firmly. "You're family."

The word settled over Daphne like a warm blanket.

Family.

She hadn't expected to find it here. She hadn't expected to feel it so deeply.

When she returned to the guest room, the moon was high in the sky, casting a soft glow through the window. She lay on the bed, staring at the ceiling, her mind full but no longer chaotic. She closed her eyes. Tomorrow, she would read the journal. But tonight, she let herself rest.

CHAPTER 16

Daphne woke to the soft clatter of dishes and the low murmur of voices drifting from the kitchen. For a moment she lay still, letting the morning light settle over her like a warm blanket. Her body felt heavy, but her mind was clearer than it had been in days. The truth had cracked something open inside her — painful, yes, but also strangely steadying.

She sat up slowly. The guest room was bright, the window open to a breeze carrying the scent of thyme and sea salt. She could hear Evanthia's voice — calm, measured — and Yannis's deeper tone responding in short, gentle bursts. They weren't whispering. They weren't tense. They were simply… talking.

Daphne stood, smoothed her hair, and stepped into the hallway.

When she entered the kitchen, both Evanthia and Yannis looked up. Evanthia's expression softened immediately.

"Good morning," she said. "Sit. Eat."

The table was set with fresh bread, cheese, a small dish of honey and a jar of marmelade. Simple, warm, inviting. Daphne sat, and Yannis pushed a plate toward her.

"You slept well," he said. His English was smooth, lightly accented, the consonants softened in a way Daphne found comforting. "That's good."

She nodded, tearing a piece of bread. "I didn't mean to sleep so long."

"You needed it," Evanthia said. "Yesterday was… a lot."

Daphne gave a small, grateful smile. "Thank you. For everything."

Evanthia waved a hand, but her eyes softened. "Eat."

They ate quietly for a few minutes, the kind of silence that felt comfortable rather than strained. Daphne watched the way Evanthia moved — efficient, calm — and the way Yannis teased her lightly about the bread being too dark on the bottom. Evanthia swatted his arm with a dish towel, and Daphne felt something warm bloom in her chest. This was what family looked like. Messy. Imperfect. Real. When the plates were mostly empty, Daphne set down her fork.

"I'm ready," she said.

Evanthia looked up. "Ready for what?"

"To read the journal."

The room stilled. Yannis's expression shifted — not tense, but attentive.

"Are you sure?" Evanthia asked.

"Yes," Daphne said. "I want to know everything there is to know."

Evanthia nodded slowly. "Let's go together."

They moved to the small room where the box still sat on the bed. The morning light fell across the quilt, illuminating the wooden lid. Daphne sat, lifted the box onto her lap, and opened it. The journal lay inside, the leather soft and worn. Daphne opened it — then paused. The handwriting was beautiful, looping, unmistakably Greek.

She swallowed. "I… I need help."

Yannis stepped closer. "Let me read it to you. And translate."

Daphne nodded. "Please."

He pulled up a chair beside her, the journal resting between them. Evanthia sat on the edge of the bed, her hands folded tightly in her lap.

Yannis cleared his throat and began reading in Greek — the words flowing smoothly, the vowels rounded, the rhythm steady. Daphne didn't understand the language, but she felt the weight of it, the intimacy of hearing her grandfather's voice through someone else's.

Then Yannis translated, his English careful, a few consonants softened, one or two words slightly mispronounced — *"ex-hausted"* becoming *"ex-hosted"* — but Daphne understood every syllable.

"The sea is loud tonight. I can't sleep. I keep thinking of the things I've broken and the things I still might save."

Daphne felt her breath catch.

Yannis continued. He read about the island — the cliffs, the olive groves, the way the wind changed before a storm. He read about the feud, translating the Greek phrases with precision. He read about Evanthia's mother with tenderness and regret, and about the fear that he was becoming a man who hurt the people he loved most.

Daphne felt her throat tighten.

"Go on," she whispered.

Yannis turned the page.

The next entry shifted — not to America, but to Perigiali, where her grandfather had been traveling regularly for months.

Yannis read the Greek first, then translated:

"I went to Perigiali again today. The quiet there helps. The distance helps. She understands that without my having to explain it. I found a house for her and for my daughter. I wish we could live here, the three of us, away from the hate and the

gossip. But even if we can't, I want to buy it for them. The least I can do is offer them some peace."

Daphne looked up. "This house."

Evanthia nodded.

Yannis continued reading.

"She asked if I was eating enough. I told her yes. She didn't believe me. She never does. She worries too much."

Daphne felt a small ache in her chest, and a hint of jealousy.

Yannis turned another page.

"Elpida mentioned going to America again. She asked if I have thought more about going. I told her I think about it every day. She didn't press."

Daphne swallowed. "My grandmother," she whispered.

Evanthia nodded. "Your grandmother," she repeated.

Yannis continued. He read about the preparations — the secrecy, the fear, the guilt. He read about the night her grandfather planned to leave the island, the way the sea looked under the moonlight, the way he felt both terrified and hopeful.

Then he reached a name he pronounced carefully, as if unsure whether Daphne would recognize it.

"Nikolas."

Daphne frowned. "Nikolas?"

Yannis translated:

"I saw Nikolas again today. I told him about the house. He is the only one who knows. The only one I trust."

Evanthia leaned closer. "I don't know that name."

Yannis shook his head. "Neither do I."

Daphne felt a spark of curiosity — sharp, insistent.

"Keep going."

Yannis turned the page.

"He says the island is changing. That people are leaving. That the old ways are dying. I told him I'm not like those people, leaving in search of opportunity. I reminded him why I'm leaving. He said he understood. Did he? He asked if I would ever come back. I told him I didn't know."

Daphne looked up. "Who was he?"

"I don't know," Evanthia said. "But he clearly mattered to your grandfather."

Yannis closed the journal gently. "There is more. But maybe… enough for now."

Daphne nodded, overwhelmed but steady. "Yes. Enough."

Yannis placed the journal back in the box and closed the lid.

"I want to know who Nikolas is," he said. "I'm going to ask around. There are people who remember things."

Daphne stood, feeling a new steadiness in her chest. "I'm going outside for a moment."

She stepped into the sunlight, the air warm against her skin. The sea shimmered in the distance, the same sea her grandfather had looked at when he was young. She closed her eyes.

"I'm trying grandpa," she whispered. "But I didn't expect you to have so many secrets. Did I ever really know you?"

The breeze lifted her hair, soft and warm, as tears slipped down her cheeks.

CHAPTER 17

Daphne stayed outside for a few more minutes, giving her eyes time to lose their swelling from the tears. When she stepped back inside, Evanthia and Yannis were clearing the breakfast dishes. Evanthia looked up immediately.

"Better?" she asked.

Daphne nodded. "Yes. I think so."

Yannis leaned his hip against the counter, arms crossed loosely. "Whenever you're ready to look at the journal again, just let me know."

Daphne appreciated the gentleness in his tone. "Yes, definitely. I can't do it without you."

Evanthia hesitated, then said, "There is something else you should see. Something I haven't looked at in a very long time."

Yannis straightened. "You mean the big box?"

Evanthia nodded slowly. "Yes. The big box."

Daphne felt a flicker of curiosity. "What big box?"

Evanthia wiped her hands on a towel. "Come. It's in the storage room."

She led them through the main room to a narrow door near the back of the house. It opened with a soft creak into a small, cluttered space filled with old baskets, folded linens, and boxes stacked haphazardly on wooden shelves.

Evanthia pointed to a box on the highest shelf — a plain cardboard one, edges softened by time.

"That one," she said. "I haven't opened it in years."

Yannis reached up easily and pulled it down. Dust puffed into the air as he set it on the table.

"What's inside?" Daphne asked.

Evanthia exhaled slowly. "Loose papers. Drawings. Notes. I found them when Yannis was small. I didn't understand them."

Daphne felt her pulse quicken. "Drawings of what?"

"A mechanism," Evanthia said. "Something he designed. Something he built."

Daphne blinked. "Built? Where?"

Evanthia looked toward the floor, then back at Daphne. "In the basement."

Daphne stared at her. She thought of the second sketch in her grandfather's letter — the rough floor plan with the steps and the dot at their base. "There's a basement?" she asked.

"Yes," Evanthia said. "It's really small. My mother never used it. I never used it. But he left some things there."

Yannis opened the box. Inside were dozens of loose sheets — some folded, some rolled, some crinkled at the edges. Daphne reached for the top one.

It was a sketch — precise, detailed, drawn in her grandfather's careful hand. Lines intersected at angles she didn't immediately understand. Arrows indicated movement. Small notes in Greek filled the margins.

Yannis leaned over her shoulder. "These are... complicated," he murmured. "Very."

Daphne traced a line with her finger. "He drew all this?"

"Yes," Evanthia said. "I recognized his handwriting. I recognized the shape of something he had built downstairs. But I didn't understand it. And I didn't want to."

"Why not?" Daphne asked.

Evanthia's expression tightened. "Because I had spent my whole life trying not to live in the shadow of his choices. I didn't want to dig into something that belonged to a part of him I never knew. And honestly, even if I tried, it seemed too complex."

Daphne nodded slowly. Yannis lifted another sheet — this one showing a cross-section of what looked like a cylindrical chamber with gears along the sides.

"This is not a hobby project," he said. "This is… engineered."

Daphne leaned closer. "I am not totally unfamiliar with this."

Evanthia and Yannis both gave her a puzzled look, but Daphne didn't look up. She sifted through the papers. Some were diagrams. Some were calculations. Some were sketches of the same object from different angles.

Yannis cleared his throat. "We should look in the basement."

Evanthia hesitated. "It's dusty. And dark. And probably full of spiders."

Yannis gave her a look. "We'll survive."

Daphne gathered the papers carefully and placed them back in the box. "Let's go."

Yannis ran to the kitchen and grabbed a lantern from a cabinet. Evanthia led them to a small door near the back of the house — one Daphne had assumed was just another storage closet. Evanthia pulled it open, revealing a narrow staircase descending into darkness. A cool draft rose from below.

"I'll go first," Yannis said.

Daphne followed, the box of papers tucked under her arm. Evanthia came last, her hand gripping the railing tightly. The stairs creaked under their weight. The air grew cooler as they descended. At the bottom was a small, low-ceilinged room with stone walls and a dirt floor. Dust coated everything — shelves, crates, an old workbench. In the center of the workbench stood something covered by a heavy cloth.

Daphne's breath caught.

Yannis lifted the lantern higher. "What is that?"

Evanthia swallowed. "The mechanism."

Daphne stepped forward slowly.

Evanthia continued, "I remember seeing it once. Just once. I didn't understand it then. I still don't."

Daphne set the box down and reached for the cloth.

"Wait," Yannis said gently. "Let me."

He grasped the edge of the cloth and pulled it back.

The lantern light fell across metal — intricate, interlocking, beautifully crafted. Gears. Levers. A cylindrical chamber like the one in the drawings. It looked old, but not crude. Functional. Intentional.

Daphne felt a shiver run through her.

"What is it?" whispered Yannis.

Evanthia shook her head. "I don't know."

Yannis stepped closer, examining the gears. "This isn't random. He built it for a purpose."

"He left us clues," Daphne said softly. "He wanted us to understand this. He left me some clues too, in another notebook."

"There is another notebook?" asked Yannis, startled.

"Yes, I have it in my suitcase, at the guesthouse. But those drawings were different, as if they described another mechanism."

"How many mechanisms are there?" asked Evanthia, her tone edged with exasperation.

Daphne didn't answer. She didn't know. Not yet. But she intended to find out.

CHAPTER 18

For a long moment, none of them spoke. The lantern rested on the bench, casting shifting shadows across the metal structure. Dust motes drifted through the beam of light, swirling like tiny ghosts. Daphne felt the air grow colder the longer she stared at the mechanism.

Yannis crouched beside it, running his fingers lightly along one of the gears. "This is not amateur work," he murmured. "He knew exactly what he was doing."

Evanthia stood a few steps back, arms wrapped around herself. She looked smaller in the dim light, as if the past had suddenly grown too close.

"I told you," she said quietly. "I didn't understand it then. I don't understand it now."

"Let's look at the drawings again. I'll run up and get the box," Yannis said. In the meantime, Evanthia and Daphne did not say a single word. They stood there in quiet awe, amazed at the intricate object in front of them.

When Yannis came back down, he and Daphne knelt on the floor and opened the box of drawings. They spread several sheets across the dirt floor. The sketches were meticulous — cross-sections, angles, measurements, annotations in her grandfather's neat Greek handwriting. Some pages showed the mechanism from above, others from the side, others from inside.

They leaned over the drawings. "He labeled everything," Yannis said. "But the labels are…impossible to understand."

Daphne pointed to a note written in the margin of one page. "What does that say?"

Yannis squinted, then read aloud in Greek before translating. "It says: *'Rotation must be steady. No sudden force.'*"

Daphne frowned. "Rotation of what?"

Yannis tapped the cylindrical chamber. "Probably this."

Evanthia stepped closer, though she still kept her distance from the machine itself.

Daphne looked up at her. "Did he ever tell you what it was for?"

"No," Evanthia said. "He didn't talk about it. Not even to my mother."

Yannis picked up another drawing. "This one shows… something moving inside the chamber."

Daphne leaned closer. "What kind of something?"

"I'm not sure," Yannis said. "It looks like… a weight? Or a counterbalance?"

He traced the lines with his finger. "See here? This part shifts when the gear turns."

"This is definitely not just decorative," he added. "It's functional."

Evanthia exhaled shakily. "He always had ideas. He was always building things. But this…" She shook her head. "This was different. He kept it hidden."

Daphne studied the mechanism again. The metal was tarnished but sturdy. The gears were thick, the levers solid. It looked like something meant to endure.

"Why would he hide it?" she asked.

Evanthia hesitated. "Maybe he didn't want anyone to know he was working on it. Or maybe he didn't want anyone to ask questions he couldn't answer."

Yannis stood and brushed dust from his hands. "We need more light."

He climbed the stairs again and returned with two more lanterns. When he lit them, the room brightened enough for Daphne to see the mechanism clearly for the first time.

It was beautiful.

Not in a delicate way — in a purposeful, almost mathematical way. Every piece fit perfectly with the next.

Every angle was intentional. Every gear was aligned with precision.

Daphne felt a strange pull in her chest. "He spent so much time on this."

"Yes," Evanthia said. "He did."

Yannis picked up a small metal handle attached to the side of the mechanism. "This looks like it turns."

Daphne's breath caught. "Should we… try it?"

Evanthia stepped forward quickly. "No. Not yet. We don't know what it does."

Yannis nodded. "She's right. We should understand it first."

Daphne looked at the drawings again. One page caught her eye — a sketch of the mechanism with a series of arrows showing movement. She pointed to a line of text written beneath it.

"What does that say?"

Yannis read it in Greek, then translated. "*'Balance must be perfect. If not, the sequence fails.'*"

"Sequence?" Daphne repeated. "What sequence?"

Yannis shook his head. "I don't know."

Evanthia rubbed her arms. "This is making me nervous."

Daphne stood and placed a hand gently on her aunt's shoulder. "We don't have to figure it out today."

Evanthia gave a small, grateful nod. But Daphne wasn't ready to leave yet. She walked slowly around the mechanism, studying it from every angle. The cylindrical chamber had a small opening at the top — barely wide enough for a hand. The gears along the side were thick and heavy, designed to bear weight. A narrow metal rod extended from the base, anchored into the floor.

"Yannis," she said quietly. "Look at this."

He joined her. "That's… unusual."

"What is it?" Evanthia asked.

Yannis crouched. "This rod goes into the ground. It's not just sitting here. It's anchored."

Daphne felt a shiver. "Anchored for what?"

Yannis didn't answer. He didn't know. But the question hung in the air like a warning.

Evanthia looked at the machine with a mixture of fear and sorrow. "I don't want it to be something dangerous."

Daphne shook her head. "I don't think it is."

"How can you know?" Evanthia asked.

"Because he wasn't a man who built things to hurt people," Daphne said softly.

Evanthia nodded slowly.

The three of them stood in silence, the lanterns casting long shadows across the stone walls.

Finally, Yannis said, "Let's take the drawings back upstairs. Study them in better light."

Daphne agreed. Evanthia exhaled, relieved. "Good. Let's go."

They gathered the papers carefully, placing them back in the box. Yannis covered the mechanism again, though the cloth now seemed too thin, too flimsy to hide something that suddenly felt so important. As they climbed the stairs, Daphne glanced back one last time. The lantern light flickered over the cloth, and for a moment she imagined she saw the gears shift beneath it — a trick of the light, surely, but enough to send a chill down her spine.

When they reached the top of the stairs, Evanthia closed the door firmly.

Daphne stood in the kitchen, the box of drawings in her arms, her pulse still unsteady. She didn't know what the mechanism was and why her grandfather built it. But she was almost certain that it was the reason her grandfather had sent her to Lefkada.

CHAPTER 19

Daphne set the box of drawings on the kitchen table. She sat first, pulling the box toward her. Yannis took the chair beside her, and Evanthia hovered for a moment before sitting across from them, her hands folded tightly in her lap.

For a moment, no one spoke. The silence wasn't heavy — just full. Full of questions, full of possibilities, full of the strange electricity that comes when the past suddenly feels alive again.

Daphne opened the box and spread the drawings across the table. The papers rustled softly, some edges curling upward as if eager to be read.

Yannis leaned forward. "Let's start with the simplest one."

He picked up a sheet showing a clean side view of the mechanism. The lines were crisp, the proportions exact. He read the Greek annotations aloud, then translated for Daphne.

"'Primary rotation axis.'
'Counterweight chamber.'
'Stabilizing arm.'"

Daphne frowned. "It sounds like something that needs to stay balanced."

Evanthia shifted in her seat. "He was always careful with balance. Even when he cooked. Even when he tied knots. He said balance was the difference between something working and something falling apart."

Daphne looked at her. "Did he ever talk about building something like this?"

"No," Evanthia said. "Never."

Yannis picked up another sheet — this one more complex, filled with arrows and numbered steps.

"This looks like instructions," he said.

Daphne leaned closer. "Can you read it?"

Yannis nodded and began translating.

"'Step one: secure the base.'
'Step two: align the chamber.'
'Step three: insert the weight.'"

He paused.

"Weight?" Daphne repeated. "What kind of weight?"

Yannis shook his head. "It doesn't say."

He scanned the rest of the page.

"'Step four: maintain even pressure on the weight.'
'Step five: rotate the mechanism slowly until it engages.'"

Daphne felt a chill. "This sounds… delicate."

"Yes," Yannis said. "Very."

Evanthia rubbed her arms. "I don't like this."

Daphne reached across the table and touched her hand. "We don't have to do anything with it. We're just trying to figure out what it's for."

Evanthia nodded, though her expression remained tense.

Yannis picked up another sheet — this one older, the ink faded, the edges frayed. It showed the mechanism from a different angle, with a long note written in Greek along the bottom. Yannis read it aloud, then translated slowly, carefully.

"'If the balance is wrong, the mechanism will fail. If the balance is right, it will reveal what must be revealed.'"

Daphne felt her breath catch. "Reveal?"

Evanthia stiffened. "Reveal what?"

Yannis shook his head. "It doesn't say."

Daphne stared at the drawing. "He built this to reveal something."

Evanthia stood abruptly, pacing a few steps before turning back to them. "I don't like this," she said again. "I don't like secrets. I don't like hidden things. I don't like the idea that he left something behind that we don't understand."

Yannis spoke gently. "Mama… we don't have to do anything with it. We're just trying to understand."

Evanthia opened her eyes. "I know. I know." She sat again, though her hands still trembled slightly.

Daphne returned to the table and picked up a small folded sheet she hadn't noticed before. It was tucked between two larger drawings, almost hidden.

She unfolded it carefully.

It wasn't a diagram.

It was a note.

Written in her grandfather's hand.

Yannis leaned in and read the Greek aloud, then translated.

"'If you are reading this, then you know about the mechanism. Do not be afraid of it. It is not meant to harm. It is meant to protect. But it must be used with care. Only when the time is right.'"

Daphne felt her heart thud.

"Protect what?" she whispered.

Yannis shook his head. "It doesn't say."

Evanthia's voice was barely audible. "I don't want to know."

Daphne looked at her gently. "But I do."

Evanthia met her eyes — and for the first time, Daphne saw not resistance, but fear. Fear of reopening wounds. Fear of discovering something she wasn't ready for. But she also saw something else: trust.

Evanthia exhaled slowly. "Then we will find out. Together."

Yannis gathered the drawings into a neat stack. "We should organize these. Try to understand the order. The sequence."

Daphne agreed. "Yes."

Evanthia stood and placed a hand on the box. "But not today."

Daphne looked at her. "Are you sure?"

"Yes," Evanthia said. "We need time. And food. And air."

Yannis smiled faintly. "She's right."

Daphne nodded.

They cleaned the table slowly, carefully, as if the papers were fragile relics — which, in a way, they were. When the last drawing was placed back in the box, Daphne closed the lid gently.

As they stepped outside, Daphne glanced back at the box on the table. She thought of the metal piece in her velvet pouch. Could there be a similar one in this mechanism? What was its significance? She hadn't mentioned it to Evanthia or Yannis yet. But she was ready to do so. Perhaps they could help her find the answer.

CHAPTER 20

The afternoon light was warm and bright when they stepped outside, but Daphne barely felt it. Her mind was still in the basement — in the dim lantern glow, in the dust, in the strange metal shape that seemed to hum with purpose even beneath the cloth. She followed Evanthia and Yannis to the small stone patio behind the house. The olive trees rustled softly in the breeze, their silver leaves shimmering.

Evanthia sank into a chair, rubbing her temples. "I need a moment," she murmured.

Yannis set the box of drawings on the table and sat beside her. Daphne remained standing, pacing slowly, her thoughts racing. The mechanism. The drawings. The note.

It is meant to protect. But it must be used with care.

Protect what?

She turned toward Yannis. "Do you think that man would know? The man grandfather mentioned in his diary? What was his name?"

Evanthia exhaled slowly. "Nikolas. I don't know who he is so I have no idea if he would know about the device." Then, hesitantly, she added, "But I might know someone who would."

Yannis turned to her. "Who?"

Evanthia explained, "There's an old man in the village. Vangelis. He's in his eighties now. He knew everyone. He remembers everything. If anyone knows who Nikolas was, it's him."

Daphne felt a spark of hope. "Can we talk to him?"

"Not today," Evanthia said gently. "He probably rests in the afternoons, and we shouldn't bother him in the evening. But tomorrow morning, yes."

Daphne nodded, trying to be patient.

Evanthia stood slowly. "I'll make coffee."

She disappeared into the house, leaving Daphne and Yannis alone on the patio.

For a moment, neither spoke.

Then Yannis said quietly, "You're not afraid."

Daphne looked at him. "Should I be?"

He shook his head. "No. But most people would be. Finding something like that in their family home… something hidden, something mechanical, something with instructions and warnings… most people would panic."

Daphne smiled faintly. "Maybe I'm not most people."

"No," Yannis said. "You're not."

She sat across from him, folding her hands on the table. "I'm not afraid because… I don't think he built it to hurt anyone. He was a kind-hearted man. He had secrets, yes, but he was a good man."

Yannis nodded slowly. "I think so too."

Daphne looked at the box of drawings. "Do you think he meant for us to find it?"

Yannis considered this. "Maybe not us specifically. But someone. Someone who cared enough to look."

Daphne felt a warmth in her chest — not comfort, exactly, but recognition. "He trusted the future more than he trusted himself."

Yannis tilted his head. "What do you mean?"

"He wrote in his diary that he couldn't fix the past," Daphne said. "But maybe he thought someone else could. Someone who wasn't tangled in the feud. Someone who wasn't carrying the guilt."

Yannis's expression softened. "You."

Daphne looked down at her hands. "I don't know. Maybe."

Evanthia returned with three small cups of Greek coffee, the aroma rich and earthy. She set them on the table and sat again, her shoulders still tense.

"We should talk about something else," she said. "Just for a little while."

Daphne nodded. "Okay."

But the mechanism lingered in her mind like a shadow. And so did the metal cylinder in her velvet pouch.

They drank their coffee in silence, the kind that wasn't uncomfortable but wasn't peaceful either. It was the silence of people thinking too much, feeling too much, trying to make sense of something that didn't yet have edges.

After a few minutes, Evanthia spoke again.

"There's something I remembered," she said quietly.

Daphne leaned forward. "What is it?"

Evanthia hesitated. "It might be nothing. But… when I was a girl, before he left, I remember him talking to someone outside the house. A man. I didn't see his face. I only heard the voices."

Daphne's pulse quickened. "Do you remember anything they said?"

"Not much," Evanthia said. "But I remember my father saying, 'It's not ready yet.' And the man said, 'It has to be.'"

Daphne felt a chill. "Do you think that man was Nikolas?"

"I don't know," Evanthia said. "But it could have been."

Yannis leaned forward. "Did your mother know about this?"

Evanthia shook her head. "If she did, she never said."

Daphne stared at the olive trees, her mind racing. "If he was talking about the mechanism… then he was building it before he left. Long before."

"Yes," Yannis said. "Which means it wasn't a last-minute idea. It was planned."

Daphne nodded slowly. "Was he able to finish it before he left? Or are we trying to understand something that isn't even finished?"

Yannis looked at her. "I really don't know." After a few seconds of silence, he stood up abruptly and pulled his phone from his pocket, his expression sharpening with purpose. "I'm going to try to find NIkolas," he said. "We found his name in Papou's notebook, more than once. He wasn't just a neighbor or someone from the village. He was someone Papou trusted."

Daphne felt her pulse quicken. "Do you think he'll talk to us?"

Yannis shrugged. "I don't know. But I want to meet him. I have questions."

"If you don't find anyone who knows him, tomorrow we can try to find Vangelis," Evanthia reminded him.

Yannis stepped inside, pacing slowly as he scrolled through his contacts. Daphne and Evanthia stayed outside, listening through the open window as he made a series of short calls — to a friend, to a fisherman he knew, to a man who ran a small taverna in the north.

Each call was brief, but with each one, Yannis's voice grew more certain.

Finally, he stopped pacing.

"I have an address," he shouted through the window. "He lives near Agios Nikitas. On the other side of the island."

Evanthia's eyes widened. "Near Kalamitsi! Where your grandfather was from!"

"Yes," Yannis said. "He's always lived there."

Daphne felt a strange tug in her chest — anticipation mixed with something heavier. "Are you going to call him?"

Yannis nodded. "I think I should."

He sat at the table, took a breath, and dialed the number he'd been given. The phone rang once. Twice. Three times. Then a voice answered — old, rough, but steady.

"Ναι;" Yes?

Yannis straightened. "Kyrie Nikola… hello. My name is Yannis—"

He didn't finish. He waited for a response, but the line went silent. Completely silent.

Yannis tried again, gently. "Kyrie Nikola? Can you hear me?"

A long breath came through the speaker. Then another. Finally, the old man spoke — his voice lower, almost hoarse.

"Yannis… whose son are you?"

"My mother is Evanthia," Yannis said. "From Perigiali."

Another silence. Then a soft, stunned exhale.

"Evanthia," the old man repeated. "Then you are… you are his grandson."

Yannis swallowed. "Yes. I found your name in one of his notebooks. Several times. I realized you must have been a good friend. Someone he trusted."

The line crackled softly. Nikolas didn't speak. He didn't breathe. He simply existed in that silence, as if the world had narrowed to a single point.

Yannis continued carefully. "I would like to meet you. I never met my grandfather, and I have many questions. I thought… maybe you could help me."

A long pause.

Then Nikolas inhaled sharply. "I will visit. Soon."

Yannis hesitated, then pressed gently. "Could you come… this week perhaps?"

Another silence.

Yannis continued, his voice steady but warm. "My cousin is here too — his other grandchild. She came from the United States. It would be a good opportunity for you to meet us both."

Another breath came through the line — this one softer, almost fragile.

"For both of you," Nikolas said quietly, "I will come."

Daphne felt her breath catch.

"I will travel to Perigiali," Nikolas continued. "Tell me where to go."

Yannis gave him their address.

"I know exactly where it is," Nikolas said. "I will come before the week ends, I promise you."

The line clicked softly as he hung up. Yannis lowered the phone.

"He's coming," he said.

Daphne felt something shift inside her — a quiet certainty, a sense of direction. The past was no longer a shadow. It was coming toward her. And she was ready.

CHAPTER 21

Nikolas arrived two days later. The morning was warm, the air soft with the scent of basil and oregano drifting in from the garden. Daphne was in the kitchen with Evanthia, slicing fruit for breakfast, when they heard a car engine outside — slow, hesitant, unfamiliar.

Yannis, who had been pacing near the window for the past thirty minutes, froze.

"That's him," he said quietly.

Daphne wiped her hands on a towel, her heart thudding. Evanthia stood very still, her expression unreadable. They stepped outside together. A small, weathered car was parked at the edge of the driveway. The driver's door opened slowly, and an elderly man stepped out — tall, though slightly stooped, with a full head of white hair and a face lined deeply, not with bitterness but with years. He looked around the yard as if searching for something he had lost long ago. Then his eyes landed on Yannis. He stopped.

Yannis stepped forward. "Kyrie Nikola?"

The old man stared at him — really stared — as if trying to reconcile the young man in front of him with a memory he had carried for decades.

"You have his eyes," Nikolas said softly. "Not just the color, but the way they look at the world."

Yannis swallowed. "I'm glad you came."

Nikolas nodded once, slowly. "I said I would."

His gaze shifted to Daphne. "And you," Nikolas said, his voice trembling. "You must be the other one."

Daphne stepped forward. "I'm Daphne."

Nikolas looked between them, his expression softening into something fragile and unbearably human.

"I never thought I would meet his grandchildren," he said. "Not in this life."

Daphne looked at Yannis, hoping for a translation. Nikolas understood and repeated in broken English what he had just said.

Evanthia stepped forward then. Nikolas smiled. "I remember you. Many years ago, you were standing on those steps just as you are now."

"I think I remember you too," Evanthia said, her voice gentle. "Come inside. Sit. You've had a long drive."

Nikolas nodded gratefully and followed them into the house. He moved slowly, not from weakness but from the weight of memory pressing on him with every step.

They settled around the kitchen table. Evanthia poured him a glass of water. His hands trembled slightly as he took it.

For a moment, no one spoke. Then Nikolas looked at Yannis. He spoke in English so Daphne could understand, though with his limited vocabulary and strong accent, he knew it wouldn't be easy for her.

"You said on the phone you found my name in his notebook."

"Yes," Yannis said. "More than once."

Nikolas nodded, his eyes distant. "We served together in the army, you know. Not in war — just service. But those years… they make men close. Closer than brothers."

Daphne felt her throat tighten.

Nikolas continued, his voice softening. "He was the bravest man I ever knew. Not because he fought. Because he loved. Because he carried things no one else could carry."

He paused, his breath catching.

"And now… now I must ask you something."

Yannis leaned forward. "Anything."

Nikolas's voice dropped to a whisper.

"Is he alive?"

The room stilled. Daphne felt the air shift — heavy, expectant, aching. Nikolas looked at Daphne, then at Evanthia, then back at Yannis. Yannis lowered his gaze.

"He passed away," Daphne said, "a couple of months ago, in Astoria, New York."

Nikolas didn't move. Not at first. He simply stared at Daphne, as if the words had not yet reached him. Then his face crumpled. Not dramatically. Not loudly.

Just a slow, devastating collapse of expression — the kind that comes from a grief carried too long and released too late. He covered his face with one hand.

"My brave days are over," he whispered. "When we were young, we weren't supposed to cry. Men didn't cry. Not then."

A tear slid down his cheek.

"But I don't mind crying now."

Another tear.

"He was my best friend. Closer than a brother."

Daphne felt her own eyes burn. She reached out and placed her hand gently over his. He didn't pull away.

Evanthia stood behind him, her hand resting lightly on his shoulder. Yannis sat very still, his jaw tight, his eyes shining.

Nikolas wiped his face with the back of his hand, embarrassed but not ashamed.

"I should have gone to him," he said. "I should have visited. I should have—"

He stopped, unable to continue.

Daphne shook her head softly. "I am sure he never blamed you."

Nikolas looked at her, eyes red. "How do you know?"

"Because he loved you like a brother," Daphne said. "He wrote about you in his journal. With respect. With affection."

Nikolas closed his eyes, breathing shakily. After a long moment, he straightened, gathering himself with the dignity of a man who had lived a full life and carried its weight.

"You said you had questions," he said to Yannis.

"Yes," Yannis replied. "Many."

"And we found something," added Daphne. "Something he built."

Nikolas inhaled slowly, deeply.

"Then it is time," he said. "Time for you to know what he was working on. Time for you to understand the mechanism."

Daphne felt her pulse quicken. "You know about the mechanism!" she exclaimed.

Yannis leaned forward. Evanthia sat down, her hands clasped tightly.

Nikolas looked at each of them in turn. "I will tell you everything," he said. He placed his hand on the table, steady now.

"Bring me the drawings," he said. "And I will show you how to read them."

CHAPTER 22

Evanthia brought the box of drawings to the table with both hands, carrying it with the kind of care one usually reserved for something fragile or sacred. She set it down gently in front of Nikolas. The old man stared at it for a long moment, his fingers hovering above the lid as though he were afraid that touching it might disturb something long buried. Daphne watched him closely. His face had settled into a quiet, solemn expression—not grief now, but something deeper, something that looked like reverence mixed with the weight of memory.

Finally, he lifted the lid.

The papers rustled softly as he sifted through them, his hands surprisingly steady for someone his age. He pulled out the first sheet—a clean side view of the mechanism—and held it up to the light. His breath caught, and for a moment he seemed transported somewhere far away.

"I remember this," he whispered. "We drew it together. He said the angles had to be perfect."

Daphne leaned forward, her curiosity sharpening. "You helped him design it?"

Nikolas nodded. "He had the idea. I had the hands. We worked well together." He set the first drawing down and picked up another—a top-down view with concentric circles. "This," he said, tapping the center, "is the heart of it. The chamber must stay balanced. If it tilts even a little, the sequence fails."

Yannis frowned, leaning closer. "What sequence?"

Nikolas didn't answer immediately. He studied the drawing again, his eyes narrowing with concentration, as though he were trying to recall something he had not thought about in decades. "Your grandfather was obsessed with balance," he said finally. "Not just in the mechanism. In life. In choices. In consequences."

He looked up at Daphne, and there was something almost apologetic in his gaze. "He built this because something needed to be protected. Something that could not be left in the open."

A chill moved through Daphne, subtle but unmistakable. "What needed to be protected? And from what? Or whom?"

Nikolas shook his head. "You needed to be protected. All of you. From the truth. A truth that your grandfather wanted you to learn—but only when the time was right."

He reached for another sheet—the one with the numbered steps. He read the Greek silently, his lips moving as he followed the sequence. Then he nodded. "Yes. This is correct. This is the sequence."

Yannis leaned closer. "Can you explain it?"

Nikolas pointed to the steps. "Step one: secure the base. That means the mechanism must be anchored. It cannot move."

"We saw the rod in the basement," Daphne said. "It's fixed into the ground."

Nikolas nodded. "Good. That part is done." He pointed to the next step. "Step two: align the chamber. That means the top cylinder must sit perfectly level. No tilt. No shift."

He tapped the drawing again. "Step three: insert the weight."

Daphne felt her pulse quicken. "What is the weight?"

Nikolas looked at her, his expression softening with something like affection. "The missing piece."

Yannis inhaled sharply. "So a piece is missing."

"Yes," Nikolas said. "Without it, the mechanism cannot function."

Daphne exchanged a glance with Yannis. "We haven't found it yet," Yannis said.

"You will," Nikolas said simply. "He would not have left it far."

He picked up another sheet—a cross-section of the chamber. "This is where the weight goes," he said, pointing to a narrow slot. "It must slide in smoothly. No force. If you force it, the gears will jam."

Daphne nodded slowly. "And once it's in?"

Nikolas tapped the next step. "Step four: maintain even pressure on the weight. Step five: rotate the mechanism slowly until it engages."

Yannis frowned. "Engages how?"

Nikolas smiled faintly. "You will hear it. A soft click. Like a lock opening."

Daphne felt a shiver run through her, a mixture of anticipation and dread. "And then?"

Nikolas set the drawing down and folded his hands on the table. "And then," he said quietly, "the mechanism will reveal what your grandfather wanted you to see."

Evanthia swallowed. "And you said you don't know what that is?"

Nikolas shook his head. "No. He never told me. He said it was not my burden."

He looked at Daphne with a steadiness that made her chest tighten. "It is yours."

The words settled into her like a weight—not heavy, but undeniable. She felt them in her ribs, in her throat, in the quiet space behind her sternum where fear and responsibility lived side by side. She thought of the metal piece in her pouch upstairs, the one she had carried with her since the day she left New York. Her grandfather had left it for her. He had placed it in her hands deliberately. And now, hearing Nikolas speak, she understood why. The missing piece was not lost. It was with her. It had been with her all along.

Her heart thudded. She opened her mouth, ready to speak, ready to tell them that she had it, that the search was already over. But something held her back. It wasn't secrecy. It wasn't fear of their reaction. It was the sudden, overwhelming sense that her grandfather had meant for her to be the one to place the weight into the mechanism. He had entrusted her with it. He had chosen her. And yet, she also felt the pull of honesty, the need to share the truth with the people who had welcomed her into their home and their history.

Before she could decide, Yannis spoke. "We need to find the missing piece," he said to Nikolas, unaware of the storm inside her.

Nikolas nodded. "Yes. And when you do, you must place it in the mechanism together."

Daphne blinked. "Together?"

"Yes," Nikolas said. "The mechanism was built by four hands. It must be completed by four hands."

Yannis nodded, solemn and steady. Daphne felt the words land with a quiet finality. She looked at the drawings spread across the table, at the lines and angles and notes written in her grandfather's hand. For the first time, she felt not fear, but clarity. The path forward was beginning to take shape, even if she wasn't ready to reveal her part in it just yet.

Nikolas leaned back in his chair, exhausted but steady. "I have told you what I can," he said. "The rest… the rest is for you to discover."

CHAPTER 23

The house felt different after Nikolas left. Not heavier, but charged in a way that made the air feel taut. Daphne stood in the doorway long after his car disappeared down the road, her hand resting lightly on the frame. The olive trees swayed in the breeze, their leaves whispering in a language she wished she understood. Something about the quiet made her chest tighten, as though the house itself was waiting for her to take the next step.

Behind her, Yannis was already gathering the drawings from the table, stacking them with a kind of focused determination that made the room feel smaller. "We should start looking," he said, his voice steady but edged with urgency.

Evanthia, who had been silent since Nikolas's explanation, turned sharply. "Looking for what?"

"The missing piece," Yannis said. "The weight."

Evanthia pressed a hand to her forehead, her expression tightening. "You think it's in this house?"

"Yes," Yannis replied. "Nikolas was certain. And Papou wouldn't have hidden it far from the mechanism."

Evanthia exhaled, long and slow, as though the idea itself exhausted her. "This house has too many corners."

Yannis smiled. "Then we'll check them one by one."

They spread the drawings across the table again, focusing on the cross-section of the chamber—the narrow slot where the missing piece would slide in. Yannis tapped the drawing, tracing the outline with his fingertip. "It can't be too big. Maybe the size of a hand. Maybe smaller."

Daphne nodded, though her throat tightened.

"And heavy," added Yannis. It has to act as a counterweight."

Evanthia sank into a chair, rubbing her temples.

Yannis looked at her. "Do you remember anything he hid that you never understood?"

"I was too young," Evanthia said. "The only thing hidden here that I never understood was the box — and the mechanism itself, of course. Nothing that looked like a weight."

Yannis sighed, leaning over the drawings again. "Then we'll have to search the whole house. Every drawer, every shelf, every loose floorboard."

Daphne felt her pulse quicken. The weight in her pouch seemed to grow heavier, as though it were pulling at her from across the room. She could almost feel its shape against her palm, the cool metal, the quiet certainty of it. Her grandfather had left it for her. He had placed it in her hands deliberately. And now, standing here with Yannis and Evanthia, she felt torn between the responsibility he had given her and the honesty she owed the people who had welcomed her into their lives as if she were their own. Her chest felt tight. She needed a moment—just a moment—to breathe, to think, to gather the courage she knew she would need. "I need a few minutes," she said quietly. "Just to absorb everything."

Evanthia looked concerned. "Are you all right?"

"Yes," Daphne said, though the word felt fragile. "I just need some air. I'll be back in a few minutes."

She stepped outside, closing the door gently behind her. She walked slowly toward the olive trees, her hands tucked into her pockets, her thoughts swirling. She thought of the metal cylinder that she had all along, and the guilt rose in her chest like a tide. She should have told them earlier. She should have said something the moment Nikolas mentioned the missing piece. But she had hesitated, caught between her grandfather's trust and the fear of betraying theirs.

How would they react? Would they think she had kept it from them on purpose? Would they think she had come here with secrets? The thought made her stomach twist. She didn't want to hurt them. She didn't want to break the fragile bond that had formed between them in such a short time.

But she also knew she couldn't keep the truth to herself any longer. Her grandfather had left the weight to her, yes—but he had also left her a letter and a path that had led her straight to them. He had meant for her to walk this journey, but not alone. He had meant for her to find them. To trust them. To share the burden with them.

She took a deep breath, letting the cool air steady her. She would tell them. She would tell them everything. And whatever came next, they would face it together.

When she walked back into the house, Yannis looked up immediately. "Are you ready to start looking?"

Daphne shook her head gently. "There's no need," she said. "I have the missing piece."

Both Yannis and Evanthia froze, their expressions shifting from confusion to surprise. Daphne gestured toward the table. "Please sit down. There's something I need to tell you."

They sat, silent and attentive. Daphne took a breath, feeling the weight of the moment settle around her. "You know that Papou left me a letter. You saw the sketches on its back page but you didn't read it and I never told you the content. In fact, nobody knows the content but me. The instructions grandpa gave the lawyer were that it was for my eyes only." She paused and took a deep breath. "But he didn't just leave me a letter. He also left me an object —

something no one else knows about either. At first, I thought he meant to exclude everyone. But now I'm certain that wasn't the case."

She looked at Evanthia, then at Yannis. "He didn't want Maria—my mother—or his younger son to know the truth. They would have felt betrayed. Lied to. And there's no reason for them to know anything now. This journey wasn't meant for them."

Her voice softened. "It was meant for me. And for you."

Evanthia's eyes glistened. Yannis leaned forward, listening intently.

"My grandfather wanted us to find each other," Daphne said. "He wanted us to finish what he started. Together."

"Give me a second," she said and got up. She went to the guest room and grabbed her purse. Evanthia and Yannis had remained silent. She sat back down, reached into her purse and grabbed the velvet pouch. She took out the cylinder and placed it gently on the table.

"This," she said quietly, "is the missing piece."

CHAPTER 24

Night settled over the house slowly, as if reluctant to fall. The sky deepened into a velvet blue, and the olive trees outside the window swayed in a rhythm that felt almost like breathing.

Daphne couldn't sleep. She lay in the small guest room, staring at the ceiling, listening to the soft hum of the fan and the distant sound of waves brushing the shore. She sat up, unable to stay still, and padded quietly into the hallway. A faint light glowed from the kitchen. She found Yannis sitting at the table, the drawings spread out again, his elbows resting on the wood, his head bowed in concentration.

He looked up when she entered.

"You couldn't sleep either," he said.

Daphne shook her head. "No."

He gestured to the chair beside him. "Come."

She sat, pulling her knees up slightly, the cool tile floor grounding her. "Thank you for not being angry at me," she said shyly.

"Of course I'm not angry at you. Mom isn't either. Don't doubt that for a moment. We understand completely. And honestly, I'm relieved you had the missing piece and spared us the search. Imagine turning the whole house upside down looking for something when we didn't even know what it looked like. Or worse, searching and never finding it. So yes, I'm actually glad you had it — and I'm definitely not angry."

Daphne stood, walked around the table, and hugged him. She wanted to cry but held herself back. Then she returned to her chair and sat down.

Yannis tapped the cross-section drawing on the table. "I keep thinking about what Nikolas said. About balance."

Daphne nodded. "It's not just mechanical."

"No," Yannis said. "It's symbolic. Intentional. He built this with meaning."

Daphne traced a finger along one of the lines. "I really think he meant for us to find it together. What do you think?"

Yannis didn't answer right away. He studied her face, his expression thoughtful.

"I think he knew you'd come back," he said. "And I think he hoped someone here would be ready to help you."

Daphne felt a warmth in her chest — not romantic, not dramatic, just a quiet recognition of connection.

She looked at the drawings again. "I'm scared."

Yannis nodded. "Me too."

She appreciated that he didn't pretend otherwise.

He leaned back in his chair. "But I'm also curious. And I want to understand him. Even if I never met him."

Daphne smiled softly. "You're more like him than you think."

Yannis raised an eyebrow. "How would you know?"

"Because you listen the way he did," she said softly. "You don't rush to fix anything before you understand it. You're patient when everything is complicated, when the situation is messy. You stay calm, you carry things quietly, and you make everyone around you feel a little safer just by being there."

Yannis looked down, a faint flush rising in his cheeks. "He was like that?"

"Yes," Daphne said. "Exactly like that."

They sat in silence for a moment, the kind that felt comfortable, like a shared breath.

Then Yannis reached for the cloth-wrapped weight, still lying on the table from earlier. He unwrapped it carefully. It gleamed faintly in the dim light.

"It's heavier than it looks," he said. The weight settled into his palm with surprising density. "It feels… important."

"It is," Daphne said. "It's the heart of the mechanism."

Yannis turned it over slowly. "Do you think he made this himself?"

"Probably," Daphne said. "Or maybe with Nikolas. Nikolas said they built everything together, didn't he? Every piece. And then I suppose grandpa took it with him when he left the island."

Yannis set the weight down gently. "I can't wait to see what it does."

"Tomorrow feels too soon," Daphne said. "But waiting won't make it easier."

"No," Yannis said. "It won't." He gathered the drawings into a neat stack. "We'll go down together. We'll take our time. We'll follow the steps exactly."

Daphne exhaled. "Okay."

They sat for another moment, the quiet stretching between them like a thread.

Then Yannis stood. "Try to sleep. Tomorrow will be a long day."

Daphne nodded and returned to her room. She lay down again, the moonlight creeping through the window and falling softly across her pillow. She welcomed its quiet wisdom, its calm, the way it seemed to steady her from the inside out.

CHAPTER 25

Morning arrived with a pale, gentle light. Daphne woke to the smell of coffee and the sound of Evanthia moving around the kitchen, talking quietly with Yannis. She dressed quickly and joined them.

Evanthia looked tired but composed. "Eat something," she said. "You'll need your strength."

Daphne managed a few bites of bread and honey. Yannis drank his coffee in silence, his eyes drifting toward the hallway that led to the basement door.

Finally, Evanthia spoke.

"I won't come down with you," she said. "I'll stay here. And I'll pray."

Yannis rolled his eyes. "Seriously, mom? Don't you think you're exaggerating a little? It's not like there's a bomb down there. I mean, I'm a little nervous too, but …pray?"

Daphne squeezed Evanthia's hand. "Don't worry. We'll be careful."

Evanthia nodded, though her eyes glistened.

Yannis stood. "Are you ready?"

Daphne took a breath. "Yes."

They walked down the hallway together. Yannis opened the basement door. The stairs creaked softly as they descended, the lantern light flickering against the stone walls. The basement felt colder than Daphne remembered. The air was still, heavy with the scent of stone and dust, as though the room had been waiting for this moment for years. Daphne held the wrapped weight in both hands, feeling its solid presence through the cloth. It seemed heavier now, not physically, but in meaning. Her grandfather had carried it for decades. Now it was hers to place. She felt a shiver run through her.

Yannis set the lantern on the floor and pulled the cloth away.

The mechanism gleamed in the dim light — metal, gears, angles, precision. It looked ancient and modern at the same time, like something out of a forgotten craft.

Daphne stepped closer. "It's beautiful."

Yannis nodded. "And complicated."

Daphne unwrapped the weight. She stared at it. The missing pieced, the key.

"We can't put it in yet," Yannis said gently. "We need to check the chamber first."

They examined the top cylinder, running their fingers along the edges, checking for tilt, for dust, for anything that might interfere.

"It's level," Yannis said. "Perfectly."

Daphne nodded, her breath shallow.

Yannis looked at her. "Are you ready?"

Daphne shook her head. "Yes, I am. Let's do this."

He held her gaze for a moment, then handed her the weight.

"Together," he said.

She nodded.

They stood side by side, the mechanism before them.

"Nikolas said two people are needed," Yannis murmured. "One to guide the weight into the slot, and the other to rotate the outer ring slowly. If the ring moves too fast, the gears won't align."

Daphne nodded, though her hands trembled slightly. "I'll place the weight," she said. "Papou left it to me. I think… I think he meant for me to be the one to do it."

Yannis looked up at her, his expression warm and steady. "Then I'll turn the ring. We'll do it together."

The simplicity of the words settled something inside her. She had come here alone, carrying secrets and questions she didn't know how to voice. Now she stood beside someone who shared her blood, someone who had been a stranger only days ago and yet felt impossibly familiar. She met his gaze, and for a moment they simply looked at each other, acknowledging the strange, unexpected closeness that had formed between them.

"Ready?" Yannis asked.

Daphne exhaled slowly. "Yes."

She knelt beside the mechanism, unwrapping the cloth with careful fingers. The weight gleamed softly in the lantern light, its surface smooth and cool. She held it in her palm, feeling the slight taper, the precision of its edges. Her hands shook, and she closed her eyes for a moment, steadying herself.

Yannis noticed. "You're doing fine," he said gently. "Take your time."

His voice grounded her. She opened her eyes and positioned the weight above the narrow slot in the chamber. The opening was small, almost invisible unless you knew where to look. She angled the weight carefully, aligning it with the groove.

"Start turning," she whispered.

Yannis placed both hands on the outer ring of the mechanism. He began to rotate it slowly, the metal moving with a soft, deliberate resistance. Daphne felt the chamber shift beneath her fingers, the internal gears adjusting as the slot opened just enough to receive the weight.

She lowered it gradually, guiding it millimeter by millimeter. The mechanism responded with a faint vibration, as though acknowledging the presence of the missing piece. Her heart pounded. She kept her focus steady, even as her hands trembled again.

Yannis glanced at her. "You're doing it," he said quietly. "Just a little more."

The weight slid deeper, the groove narrowing around it. Daphne felt the moment when the metal met the internal gears—an almost imperceptible click of alignment. She pressed gently, and the weight settled into place with a soft, final sound that echoed faintly in the stillness of the basement.

Yannis stopped turning the ring. They both held their breath.

For a moment, nothing happened.

Then the mechanism shuddered softly, as though waking from a long sleep. A low hum vibrated through the metal, and the chamber rotated on its own, completing the sequence Nikolas had described. Daphne stepped back, her pulse racing.

A small panel on the side of the mechanism slid open, revealing a narrow compartment. Inside was a folded piece of paper, yellowed with age but perfectly preserved.

Daphne reached for it with trembling fingers. She held it in her hands for a long moment before she could bring herself to open it. The basement felt impossibly still—the kind of stillness that follows a long-held breath, when the world waits to see what has changed. Yannis stood beside her, silent and steady, the lantern flickering softly between them. The mechanism, now quiet, seemed almost watchful, as though it had fulfilled its purpose and was waiting for her to understand what came next. She unfolded it slowly, the paper crackling softly. The edges were brittle, the ink slightly faded, but the handwriting was unmistakable—strong, deliberate, familiar in a way that made her chest tighten. Her grandfather's hand. The sight of it alone made her throat constrict. She traced the first line with her eyes.

"Of course, It's in Greek. Papou must be laughing wherever he is. You read it, Yanni." She handed the note to Yannis. He took it very carefully, respectfully.

To the one who finds this,

You are my blood. You are my family. If you have reached this moment, then the time was right. What I could not say, I leave here in truth. The past is not a burden when carried together. What was broken can be mended. What was hidden can be shared. Follow the path with courage. You are not alone.

Yannis paused. Daphne's throat tightened. She asked Yannis to read the lines again, more slowly, feeling each one settle into her like a quiet, steadying heartbeat. Her grandfather had written this long before she was born, long before he knew who would stand here. Yet somehow, impossibly, it felt like he had written it for her.

Yannis stepped closer, his voice soft. "Shall I keep going?"

"Yes, please. Read the whole thing," Daphne said.

I built this mechanism because I could not carry everything with me. Some truths must stay where they belong. Some truths must wait for the right hands.

Daphne's breath trembled. The words felt heavier than the weight they had placed inside the mechanism.

If you are here, then you are one of those hands.

Daphne blinked rapidly, fighting the sting in her eyes. Yannis touched her elbow gently, grounding her, but she shook her head. She needed to hear all of it. She crossed her arms, lowering her gaze to the floor.

I do not know who you are yet—only that you are mine. My blood. My family. And that you came back to this house for a reason.

A quiet ache spread through her chest. She felt the truth of it settle into her bones. He hadn't known her name, but he had known she would come. He had known someone would.

You will not find everything in the mechanism. It is only the beginning. A door, not a destination.

She looked up at Yannis. "A door?"

He nodded slowly. "Maybe not literal. Maybe something he meant for us to understand later."

You must look beyond the metal and the gears. Look to the people. Look to the stories that were never told. Look to the choices that shaped us.

His voice softened, almost breaking.

And look to the place where everything began.

Daphne frowned. "What place?"

Yannis shook his head. "I don't know. Maybe he explains further down."

I could not fix the past. I could only protect what mattered. If you are reading this, then the past is no longer mine to carry. It is yours now.

Yannis lowered the letter, his hands trembling now. Silence filled the basement—thick, heavy, alive. Yannis exhaled slowly, his voice gentle. "There's a little more. And I hope it's a bit more specific, because so far this has been very vague."

"Keep going," Daphne said and Yannis lifted the paper again. The final lines were shorter, written with a firmer hand.

Find Nikolas. He knows what I could not finish. Tell him to take you to the place where everything started, and to the one who started it. He has my permission now. Trust him. And trust

"It's quite cryptic," Yannis said. I think we'll have to read it once more. Or twice! So we have to talk to Nikolas again? Didn't he say that he told us everything he knew?"

"I don't think he told us everything," Daphne replied. "It seems like he needed Papou's permission to tell us."

"And this is the permission?" Yannis asked, puzzled.

"Exactly. But it's not just permission," Daphne said, extending her hand to take the paper from Yannis.

"He meant for us to find this together. He meant for us to find each other."

They stood there in the dim light of the basement, the mechanism humming softly beside them, the weight now part of the whole. The air felt different—lighter, warmer, as though the room itself had exhaled.

Daphne looked at Yannis again, and he met her gaze with the same steady warmth as before. Two people who had been strangers only days ago now stood united by blood, by history, by the quiet courage of a man who had trusted them to finish what he began.

"Thank you," she whispered.

Yannis shook his head gently. "We did it together."

Daphne pressed the letter to her chest, closing her eyes. "Thank you, Papou," she said. "Thank you for my new family."

Yannis took her hand. He smiled, and she smiled back. Then she pulled her hand away and wiped the tears from her eyes. She folded the paper and put it in her pocket. "What do you think he means by 'the place where everything started'?"

Yannis thought for a moment. "It could be the village where he grew up. Or the land he left behind. Or something else entirely."

Daphne folded the letter carefully. "We need to ask Nikolas."

"Yes," Yannis said. "We do."

She looked around the basement—the stone walls, the lantern light, the mechanism that had slept for decades. "It feels like we woke something up," she whispered.

Yannis nodded. "We did."

Daphne took a deep breath. "Let's go upstairs."

They climbed the stairs slowly, the letter held tightly in her hand. When they reached the kitchen, Evanthia stood immediately, her eyes searching their faces.

"What happened?" she asked.

Daphne held up the note. "He left this for us."

Evanthia's hand flew to her mouth. "Oh… oh my God."

Daphne stepped forward and placed the letter gently on the table. "We need to talk to Nikolas again," she said. "Soon."

Yannis nodded. "I'll call him."

Evanthia sank into a chair, tears in her eyes. "Your grandfather… he always knew someone would come back."

Daphne sat beside her, taking her hand. "He built all of this for a reason," she said. "And I think we're finally beginning to understand it."

CHAPTER 26

After the mechanism revealed the letter, a heavy tension settled in the house. Daphne sat at the kitchen table with her grandfather's note spread out in front of her. Yannis stood by the window, phone in hand, waiting for Nikolas to answer. Evanthia moved around the kitchen in slow, deliberate motions, making coffee she barely touched. She kept glancing at the note, then away again, as if afraid of what it might say if she looked too long.

Finally, Yannis lowered the phone. "He's not picking up."

Daphne folded the letter carefully. "He'll call back."

"He will," Yannis agreed. "But I think we should go to him."

Evanthia turned sharply. "Today?"

"Yes," Yannis said. "He needs to see the note. And we need answers."

Daphne nodded. "He told us to find him. Papou told us to find him."

Evanthia hesitated, her fingers tightening around her mug. "Agios Nikitas is far. The roads are narrow. It's already noon. What time will you get back? Why don't you go tomorrow?"

"Mom, it's not even an hour's drive," Yannis complained.

Daphne looked at Yannis. "She is right. This is a lot to absorb, we can use the evening to read the note again and be better prepared for whatever we're going to learn tomorrow."

"All right. We'll leave early, at six o'clock at the latest," Yannis said sharply.

Evanthia exhaled slowly. "Thank you. Don't forget he's an old man. He'll be in better shape to speak with you in the morning. And be gentle with him. He's carrying more than he lets on."

Daphne could barely sleep that night. At five-thirty in the morning, she came out of her room and headed to the kitchen for a quick cup of coffee before the drive. Yannis was sitting by the front door, tying his shoes.

"Good morning!" she said, smiling. "I see you're ready to go."

"I was ready yesterday," Yannis said. "We could have gone and come back before sunset. Honestly, I don't know why my mom worries so much."

Daphne drank her coffee faster than she'd ever had. Five minutes later, they were out the door. The drive to the other side of the island took nearly forty minutes. The road wound through hills and olive groves, past small villages. The sea appeared and disappeared between the trees, flashes of deep turquoise that made Daphne's chest ache with a strange, familiar longing.

Yannis drove with quiet focus, his hands steady on the wheel. Daphne held the letter in her lap, the paper warm from her touch.

"Are you nervous?" Yannis asked.

"Yes," she said honestly. "You?"

"Of course."

She smiled faintly. "You hide it better."

He shrugged. "I'm a man, and this is Greece. I grew up with the old village ways."

They fell into a comfortable silence. The road narrowed as they approached Agios Nikitas, the houses clustered close together, the air filled with the scent of pine and sea salt.

Yannis slowed the car. "His house should be just ahead."

Daphne leaned forward, scanning the small stone homes lining the road. Then she saw it — a modest house with a faded blue door and a small garden overflowing with basil and rosemary.

"That's it," Yannis said.

He parked the car, and they stepped out into the warm morning air. Daphne felt her heart thudding as they approached the door.

Yannis knocked gently. For a moment, nothing happened. Then the door opened.

Nikolas stood there, wearing the same simple clothes he had worn in Perigiali — a buttoned shirt, worn trousers, and an expression that softened the moment he saw them.

"You came," he said quietly.

"Yes," Yannis replied. "We need to talk."

Nikolas stepped aside. "Come in."

The inside of the house was small but warm — shelves lined with old photographs, a wooden table covered with a checkered cloth, a kettle steaming softly on the stove.

Nikolas motioned for them to sit. "You look tired," he said to Daphne.

She nodded. "It's been… a lot."

"I know," he said gently. "Your grandfather never did anything halfway."

Daphne took a breath. "We found the missing piece."

Nikolas's eyes widened slightly. "You did?"

"Yes," Yannis said. "And we put it in the mechanism."

Nikolas closed his eyes for a moment, as if absorbing the weight of that sentence. "And?"

Daphne unfolded the note and placed it on the table.

"It revealed this."

Nikolas stared at the paper. His hand trembled slightly as he reached for it. He didn't read it right away. He just held it, his thumb brushing the edge.

"His handwriting," he whispered. He read the letter slowly, carefully, his lips moving silently. When he reached the final lines, he exhaled shakily.

"I have his permission. The time has come."

Daphne swallowed. "He said the mechanism was only the beginning. That we need to look to the place where everything began."

Nikolas nodded, folding the note with reverence. "I know what he meant."

Daphne leaned forward. "Tell us."

Nikolas looked at her — really looked — and she saw something shift in his eyes. Not fear. Not hesitation. He saw resolve.

"It began in the old village," he said. "The one in the hills. The one your grandfather left behind."

Daphne frowned. "I thought he grew up here."

"No," Nikolas said. "This was where he lived later. But the beginning — the real beginning — is in the village above the cliffs. The place he never spoke about."

Yannis exchanged a glance with Daphne. "Why didn't he talk about it?"

Nikolas's voice softened. "Because that is where the story broke. And where he believed it could be mended."

Daphne felt a chill. "What happened there?"

Nikolas looked right into her eyes. "You will find out. I need to take you there."

Daphne's breath caught. "When?"

Nikolas looked out the window, toward the hills rising in the distance.

"Now," he said. "Right now." He turned back to them, his expression solemn. "If you want to understand your grandfather," he said, "you must see where he came from. And you must hear the story from the place itself."

Daphne nodded slowly. She was ready. So was Yannis.

"Let's go," Nikolas said. "The old village is waiting."

CHAPTER 27

The drive to the old village was not as smooth as Daphne was used to. But it was also more beautiful than she was used to. The narrow road wound upward through olive groves and low stone walls, the scent of thyme and wild sage drifting through the open windows with the cool morning air. Birds stirred in the branches above them, their calls echoing across the quiet hills.

Daphne sat beside Yannis in the front seat and glanced at Nikolas in the rearview mirror. "How far is it?"

"Not far," he said. "But the road is steep." He looked out the window with eyes full of nostalgia. "It's been many years since I came this way."

Daphne sensed something in his voice — not fear, not reluctance, but a kind of solemnity. As if he were returning to a place he had once loved and once lost.

They continued upward, the village below shrinking into a patchwork of rooftops and gardens. The sea glittered in the distance, a thin line of silver against the horizon.

After a while, the paved road gave way to a narrow dirt path. The air grew cooler, the trees denser. Daphne felt the shift — the way the world seemed to quiet itself as they climbed.

Yannis slowed. "It looks like we're close."

Daphne looked around. "I don't see anything."

"You will," Nikolas said.

They rounded a bend. And there it was. The old village. Or what remained of it. Stone houses, long abandoned, stood in silent clusters along the hillside. Roofs had collapsed in places, vines crawled over doorways, and wildflowers grew through cracks in the stone.

Yannis stopped the car and they all got out.

"It's beautiful," Daphne whispered.

Nikolas nodded. "It was once full of life."

Yannis looked around, his expression thoughtful. "Why did people leave?"

Nikolas exhaled slowly. "Some left for work. Some for opportunity. Some because they had no choice."

They walked toward a small stone house with a broken wooden door. The walls were cracked, but the structure still stood, stubborn and proud.

"This was his home," Nikolas said quietly.

Daphne stepped closer. The doorway was low, the threshold worn smooth by decades of footsteps. She touched the stone, feeling its coolness, its age.

"He grew up here?" she asked.

"Yes," Nikolas said. "This is where everything began."

Yannis looked around. "It's hard to imagine."

Nikolas nodded. "It was different then. Children running through the fields. Women baking bread in the outdoor ovens. Men working the land. It was a small world, but it was ours."

Daphne stepped inside the house. The interior was dim, the roof partially collapsed, but she could still see the outline of what had once been a home — a hearth, a small alcove for sleeping, a narrow window overlooking the valley.

She imagined her grandfather as a boy — barefoot, curious, full of dreams he never spoke about. She felt a tightness in her chest.

Nikolas stood in the doorway, watching her.

"He loved this place," he said. "But he also feared it."

Daphne turned. "Why?"

Nikolas hesitated.

Then he stepped inside, his cane tapping softly against the stone floor.

“There was a feud,” he said. “A long one. Between families. Between people who forgot how to forgive.”

“My mother told us about the feud,” Yannis said. “Not in detail, but we didn’t want to press. I guess she told us all she knew, or all she could.”

“Your mother cannot possibly know the whole truth. Only your grandfather did, and he told nobody but me,” Nikolas said as he walked deeper into the room, his hand brushing the wall as if greeting an old friend.

“It was a feud that lasted a very long time. It was the kind that begins with pride and ends with silence. Your grandfather was caught in the middle. He tried to mend it. He tried to bring peace. But he was young. And the old wounds were too deep.”

Daphne felt her pulse quicken. “You mean, the feud didn’t start with him? I thought he caused it.”

“Yes, by falling in love with my grandmother,” added Yannis.

Nikolas’s voice softened. “No, he was not the one who started it. He was the one who tried to end it. And so he made a choice. A choice that saved someone. And cost him something else.”

Daphne stepped closer. “Cost him what?”

Nikolas looked at her — really looked — and she saw the weight of decades in his eyes.

"His place here," he said. "His home. His family. His future. Everything he thought he would become."

Daphne felt the words settle into her like stones.

"He never told anyone," Nikolas continued. "Not even me. Not the whole story. But I know enough."

Yannis crossed his arms. "Why didn't he come back?"

Nikolas sighed. "I suppose because he built a life in America. He built a family." He smiled sadly and added, "But the past does not disappear just because we leave it behind."

Daphne looked around the small stone house — the place where her grandfather had taken his first steps, spoken his first words, dreamed his first dreams.

"What do we do now?" she asked.

Nikolas pointed toward the far end of the village, where a narrow path disappeared into the trees.

"There is someone you must meet," he said. "Someone who knows the part of the story I cannot tell."

Daphne's breath caught. "Who?"

Nikolas turned toward the path.

"His brother," he said.

Daphne froze.

"Papou had a brother?"

Nikolas nodded. "Yes. And he is still alive."

Yannis stared. "Why didn't we know this? Why didn't anyone tell us?"

Nikolas looked at them both, his expression solemn.

"Because some truths," he said, "wait for the right moment to be spoken."

He gestured toward the path.

"Come. He has been waiting a long time."

Daphne felt her heart pounding as she followed Nikolas toward the trees. Yannis put his hand on her shoulder and said softly, "I'll translate everything, don't worry." Daphne nodded, grateful.

The old village watched them go — silent, patient, full of stories that were finally ready to be heard.

CHAPTER 28

The path narrowed as they moved deeper into the trees, the air cooling, the light shifting into a soft green glow. Daphne walked behind Nikolas, her heart thudding with every step. Yannis stayed close beside her, silent but steady. The old village had felt like a memory. This path felt like a threshold.

Nikolas slowed as they approached a small clearing. A stone house stood at the far end — smaller than the others, but intact. A wooden chair sat outside the door, facing the valley below.

Someone was sitting in it.

An old man — older than Nikolas — with silver hair pulled back into a low knot, his posture straight despite his age. His hands rested on a cane carved from olive wood.

He didn't turn when they approached. He had been expecting them.

Nikolas stopped a few steps away. "Kosta."

The old man didn't move. "You brought them." His voice was low, rough, but clear.

Nikolas nodded. "Yes."

Only then did the man turn his head. His eyes — sharp, dark, impossibly alive — landed on Daphne. She felt something inside her jolt. Not recognition. But something close to it. The old man studied her for a long moment, his gaze steady, unblinking.

Daphne swallowed. "You look so much like grandfather."

He let out a soft, humorless sound. "I know."

Nikolas stepped forward. "Kosta, this is Daphne. And this is Yannis."

Kosta nodded once, acknowledging them without warmth but without hostility.

"Come," he said. "Sit."

There were two wooden stools near the doorway. Daphne and Yannis sat. Nikolas remained standing, leaning slightly on his cane.

Kosta looked at Daphne again. "You came a long way."

"Yes," she said. "I needed to understand."

Kosta's eyes narrowed. "Understand what?"

"What happened here," Daphne said. "Why he left. Why he never came back."

Kosta tapped his cane against the ground. "And you think I will tell you."

Daphne held his gaze. "I hope you will."

Kosta studied her for another long moment. Then he exhaled, a sound that carried decades.

"He was my brother," he said. "My only brother. And I loved him. Even when I hated him."

Daphne felt her breath catch. "Why would you hate him?"

Kosta looked out at the valley, his jaw tightening. "Because of what he took from me."

Nikolas stepped forward. "Kosta—"

Kosta raised a hand. "No. They came for the truth. They deserve to hear it."

He turned back to Daphne.

"You know there was a feud."

"Yes," she said. "Nikolas told us."

Kosta nodded. "But he did not tell you the heart of it."

He leaned back in his chair, the wood creaking softly.

"It began with land," he said. "As these things often do. A boundary. A dispute. Pride. Anger. Two families who refused to yield."

Daphne listened, her pulse quickening.

"Our family," Kosta continued, "and the family that lived just beyond the ridge."

Yannis frowned. "Who were they?"

Kosta's eyes hardened. "The Vrettos family."

Yannis felt a chill. "My grandma's maiden name."

"Indeed," Kosta said. "Your grandfather spent years trying to forget it, until it came back to haunt him."

Nikolas shifted uncomfortably. "Kosta—"

But Kosta ignored him.

"The feud grew," he said. "Small things became big things. Words became threats. Threats became fights. And then…"

He paused.

Daphne leaned forward. "And then what?"

Kosta's voice dropped.

"And then someone got hurt."

Silence fell over the clearing.

Daphne's heart pounded. "Who?"

Kosta looked at her — really looked — and she saw something break in his expression.

"A child," he said. "A boy from the Vrettos family."

Daphne's breath caught. "Was Papou involved?"

Kosta closed his eyes. "He was there."

Yannis stiffened. "Did he…?"

"No," Kosta said sharply. "He was not the one responsible for the boy's death. But he was blamed. And he took the blame."

Daphne stared at him. "Why?"

Kosta's voice softened, almost breaking. "Because he was protecting someone."

Daphne felt the world tilt. "Whom?"

Kosta looked away.

Nikolas stepped forward. "Kosta, you said they deserve to know the truth. You've said this much, you can't stop now."

Kosta's jaw tightened. "I know." He looked down. "He was protecting me."

Daphne froze. Yannis inhaled sharply. Nikolas closed his eyes.

Kosta continued, his voice rough. "I was the one who caused the accident. I was the one who panicked. I was the one who ran. And your grandfather… he stepped forward. He said it was him. He said he would take the blame."

Daphne felt tears sting her eyes. "Why would he do that?"

"Because he was the older brother," Kosta said. "Because he thought he could bear it. Because he believed the truth would destroy me."

He looked at her, his eyes shining with something raw.

"And because he loved me."

Daphne pressed a hand to her mouth.

Kosta continued. "The Vrettos family demanded punishment. They demanded justice. The village demanded peace. But the boy's mother couldn't bare any more pain, and she couldn't bare to live in the same village anymore. So she and her husband left. They moved to the other side of the island, to Nydri. They wanted distance, a new start, a place where no one whispered their name with pity."

The words hung in the air like smoke.

Yannis felt his chest tighten. "Did they ever have another child?"

Kosta nodded. "Yes, a girl—who grew up to become a beautiful woman and, as luck or perhaps irony would have it, met Yannis when he went to Nydri one day for business."

Daphne looked at Yannis who was shaking. "Your grandmother," she whispered. Yannis nodded.

"His grandmother, Alexandra" confirmed Kosta. "So just when everyone thought the feud was finally settling down, he stirred it up again."

Kosta's eyes softened, just barely. "Yannis fell in love with Alexandra the way only a man carrying guilt can—quietly, fiercely, with a hope he didn't think he deserved."

Daphne felt her breath catch. "And she loved him?"

"She did," Kosta said. "Enough to marry him. Enough to give him a daughter."

Yannis blinked. "Evanthia."

Kosta nodded. "Your mother," he said to Yannis. "Your grandmother Alexandra was the daughter of the Vrettos family. And your grandfather Yannis… he was the man they blamed for her brother's death."

The clearing seemed to tilt. Daphne felt the weight of the revelation settle like a stone in her stomach.

"But she didn't know," Kosta continued. "Not then. Not until later."

He paused, gripping his cane more tightly.

"While your grandfather was building a life in Nydri, I was destroying mine here."

Daphne's pulse quickened. "What do you mean?"

Kosta's jaw tightened. "I met Elpida. A good woman. Too good for me. She loved me before she understood what I had become. Before the guilt rotted me from the inside."

Daphne felt a coldness spread through her chest. "Elpida? That was my grandmother's name."

"Yes," Kosta said. "Elpida was your grandmother. And she gave me a daughter."

Daphne's breath caught. "Maria."

Kosta nodded. "Your mother."

The ground felt unsteady beneath her. She felt Yannis's hand brush her arm—not touching, but close enough to steady her.

Kosta continued, his voice cracking. "I tried to be a good man. I tried to be the man she believed I was. But guilt is a poison. It eats everything. I drank. I shouted. I broke things. I broke her trust. I broke her heart." He closed his eyes. "And then I started breaking her."

Daphne felt her stomach twist. "You hurt her."

"Yes," Kosta whispered. "I became the kind of man I swore I would never be. Violent. Angry. Unpredictable. Elpida feared for her life. And for Maria's."

Daphne felt tears sting her eyes. "Why didn't she leave?"

"She tried," Kosta said. "But she had nowhere to go. No money. No family left. And she was ashamed."

He looked at Daphne, and for the first time she saw something like remorse—deep, raw, unfiltered.

"One day," he said, "she told Yannis the truth."

"She told him you were hurting her," Daphne said.

"Yes," Kosta said. "She told him she was afraid I would kill her. And he… he did what he always did. He tried to save the people he loved."

Yannis leaned forward. "What happened?"

Kosta exhaled shakily. "He started visiting. Helping. Protecting. He became the man I should have been. And Elpida… she trusted him. She confided in him. She leaned on him."

Daphne's pulse quickened. "Did they…?"

"No," Kosta said sharply. "Not then. Not like that. But they cared for each other. And I saw it. And it made me worse."

He looked away, ashamed.

"One night," he said, "I got drunk. Drunker than usual. And when Yannis and Alexandra came to visit… I told the truth."

"The truth?" Daphne asked.

"About the boy," Kosta said. "I told them everything. That the man the Vrettos family hated was Yannis."

Yannis jumped out of his seat. "But you were the one to blame, not my grandpa!"

Kosta swallowed hard. "I was drunk, and I was angry. Bitter. Jealous."

"Alexandra realized, in that moment, that the man she loved—the father of her daughter—was the man she had been raised to despise."

Daphne felt her throat tighten. "She sent him away."

"Yes," Kosta said. "She told him to leave. She told him she could never forgive him. She told him she didn't want him near Evanthia."

Yannis closed his eyes, grief flickering across his face.

"And so," Kosta said, "he left. Not because he wanted to. Not because he had fallen in love with someone else. But because the people he loved most didn't want him around them."

 "And Elpida?" Daphne asked.

"She begged him to take her and Maria," Kosta said. "She said they could go far away. Start over. Be safe."

Daphne's voice trembled. "America."

Kosta nodded. "Yes. She told him she had a cousin there. She told him they could build a life. And he… he hesitated at first but he finally agreed. Because he cared for her. Because he wanted to save her. Because he wanted to save the child. My child."

"Your child," Daphne whispered, her heart pounding. "Maria."

Kosta looked at her, his eyes full of decades of regret.

"Maria was not his daughter," he said softly. "She was mine."

Daphne felt the world shift beneath her.

"And that," Kosta said, "means I am your grandfather."

The clearing fell silent.

Daphne stared at him, her breath caught somewhere between disbelief and grief. She felt Yannis's hand finally touch her arm, grounding her as the truth settled into her bones.

Her grandfather—the man she had loved, the man who had raised her mother, the man who told her stories and taught her how to tie knots—had not been her blood.

But he had been her family.

And the man sitting before her—the broken, remorseful, complicated man—was her real grandfather.

Kosta looked at her with eyes full of sorrow.

"You came here for answers," he said. "Now you have them."

Daphne swallowed hard, her voice barely a whisper. She felt something shift inside her—pain, yes, but also clarity.

The past had not been what she thought. But now she finally understood it.

She wiped her eyes. "Did you ever speak again? You and my grandfather?"

Kosta's voice cracked. "Once. Many years later. He wrote to me. He said he forgave me. But I never forgave myself."

There was a long moment of silence.

"And I don't expect you to forgive me," added Kosta.

No one spoke. Even the birds that had been chirping all along fell silent.

CHAPTER 29

Daphne didn't speak at first. She stood there in the clearing, the truth still echoing inside her like a bell struck too hard. The trees around them swayed gently, the morning light shifting across the stones, but everything felt strangely distant, as though the world had stepped back to give her space. Finally, she drew in a slow breath.

"I need to process this," she said quietly. "I… I can't take it all in at once."

Kosta nodded, his expression solemn. "I understand." His voice was rough, but steady. "And I will understand if you never want to see me again."

Daphne looked up sharply, but he continued before she could speak.

"I know what I became," he said. "I know what I did. I know I don't deserve forgiveness. I don't even deserve your presence here." He gripped his cane, knuckles whitening. "But I am grateful that I had the chance to meet you before I leave this world. Grateful that I could look at you once and know that something good came from all the ruin I caused."

Daphne's throat tightened. She didn't know what to say. She wasn't ready to offer forgiveness, but she wasn't ready to condemn him either. She simply nodded, and Kosta seemed to accept that as the only answer she could give.

Nikolas stepped forward, adjusting his weight on his cane. "We should go," he said gently. "We have to get back to my house, and then you two have to drive back home."

Daphne and Yannis rose from their stools. Daphne hesitated, glancing once more at the old man in the chair. Kosta didn't look at her. He stared out at the valley, as if the land itself held the last pieces of his life.

As they turned to leave, Nikolas paused beside him.

"It was good to see you again," he said softly. "After all these years."

Kosta didn't turn, but his jaw tightened. "You too, Nikolas."

There was nothing more to say. The three of them stepped back onto the narrow path, the clearing disappearing behind them as the trees closed in.

The walk back to the car was quiet. Daphne felt the weight of everything pressing against her ribs — the truth about her mother, the truth about her grandmother, the truth about the man she had called Papou her entire life. She felt hollow and full at the same time, as though her heart was trying to rearrange itself around a new shape.

When they reached Nikolas's house, he opened the door and motioned them inside. The familiar scent of herbs and old wood wrapped around them, grounding them after the long, heavy morning. Nikolas set his cane against the wall and turned to face them.

"You two need to decide something," he said. "Are you going to tell Evanthia?"

Daphne felt her stomach twist. She looked at Yannis, who was staring at the floor, his jaw tight. After a long moment, he lifted his head.

"She deserves to know," he said. "All of it. Even if it hurts."

Nikolas nodded. "Then you should tell her soon. Secrets don't get lighter with time."

Daphne swallowed. She knew he was right. But the thought of telling Evanthia — of shattering her understanding of her own parents, her own history — made her chest ache.

Nikolas looked straight into Daphne's eyes. "Will you tell your mother?" he asked softly.

Daphne felt dizzy. She took a few unsteady steps and sank into the old sofa beside her. Leaning forward, she pressed her hands against her temples. "I don't know," she said. "I don't know how she'll handle it. I don't even know how to handle it myself."

Nikolas looked at her with compassion. "Take your time. The shock will probably be much greater for Maria than for Evanthia."

Yannis stepped closer and placed a hand on her shoulder. "We'll tell Evanthia together, and I'm grateful for that. But with Maria… you'll have to do it alone. I wish I could be there with you. Still, we can plan what you'll say. We can talk it through—if you decide to tell her."

Daphne gently squeezed the hand he had resting on her shoulder.

With some effort, Daphne rose and walked slowly toward the door, Yannis following behind her.

They thanked Nikolas and stepped outside again. The sun had climbed higher, warming the path as they began the drive back toward Perigiali. The sea glittered in the distance, but Daphne barely saw it. She stayed silent for a long time, her thoughts circling the same questions over and over.

Finally, she spoke.

"Do you think… do you think this is what he wanted me to find?" Her voice was soft, almost uncertain. "The mechanism. The sketches. The letter. Do you think he wanted me to find you and Evanthia… or him?"

Yannis didn't answer right away. He kept his eyes fixed on the road ahead.

"I think," he said slowly, "that he wanted you to find the truth. All of it. Not just one piece."

Daphne looked at him.

"And the truth," Yannis continued, "is that you belong to both stories. To both families. To both men. The one who raised your mother, and the one who gave her life. I think he wanted you to know where you came from. All the way back."

"And Evanthia?" she asked.

Yannis nodded. "She deserves the truth too. Even if it hurts. Even if it changes everything."

Daphne looked down at the path beneath her feet. "We'll tell her together."

"Yes," Yannis said. "Together."

As they drove toward Perigiali, the air smelled of pine and salt, and the cicadas hummed in the trees. The world felt different now — heavier, but also clearer.

Daphne didn't know what would happen next. She didn't know how Evanthia would react, or how the truth would reshape the fragile connections they had begun to build. But she knew one thing: telling the truth would be easier than carrying the burden in silence for the rest of their lives, as her grandfather had done.

CHAPTER 30

Yannis and Daphne stepped into the house and lingered in the doorway a moment too long, as if neither of them was quite ready to move forward. The air felt unusually heavy, thick with unspoken words.

Evanthia looked up from the coffee table where she had been sorting through old photographs. She smiled when she saw them, but the smile faded almost immediately. Something in their faces told her they had something important to say—and that it was unlikely to be good news.

Evanthia brushed her hands lightly against her apron and gave them a forced, almost hurried smile. "Come," she said, her voice overly bright, "let's go to the kitchen. I made meat pie." She didn't wait for an answer, as if the simple act of serving food could postpone whatever weighed on their faces. Daphne and Yannis exchanged a quick glance but followed her without protest. Together, they walked into the kitchen, the smell of warm pastry and spices filling the room, the unspoken words trailing closely behind them.

Daphne and Yannis sat at the kitchen table, their hands resting close but not quite touching. The room felt too small, too bright, too fragile for the truth they carried. Yannis's expression was steady but tense. They had decided to tell her together, and Yannis was grateful for that. He knew he couldn't have done this alone.

"What happened?" she asked quietly.

Daphne exchanged a glance with Yannis. He nodded for her to begin, but her throat tightened. She took a slow breath.

"Evanthia," Daphne said, "we went to see Kosta."

Evanthia's expression sharpened. "Kosta? I didn't know he was still alive!" After a short pause she asked, "Why did you go see him?"

"Because he knew things," Yannis said. "Things about our families. Things we didn't understand."

Evanthia set the photographs down. "What things?"

Daphne stepped closer. "We learned the truth about the feud. About why your father left."

Evanthia's breath caught. "My father left because he fell in love with another woman."

Daphne shook her head gently. "No. That's not what happened."

Yannis sat beside her. "Your mother told you that. But it wasn't true."

Evanthia stared at him, confusion tightening her features. "What do you mean?"

Yannis took her hand. "Your father didn't leave because he wanted to. He left because your mother sent him away."

Evanthia froze.

"You know about the accident, right?" Yannis asked quietly.

"What accident?" Evanthia replied, puzzled.

"The death of your mother's older brother."

Evanthia frowned slightly. "I know a few things. My grandparents had a boy before my mother was born, but he drowned. My mother never wanted to talk about it in detail. It was too painful. I never pressed her."

Daphne and Yannis exchanged a brief glance. Then Daphne continued softly, "We learned that the drowning wasn't just a tragic accident. It was caused by Kosta. But your grandpa took the blame to protect his younger brother."

Evanthia looked at her blankly, not yet understanding where this was leading.

Yannis drew a slow breath. "Your mother never knew that either Kosta or Papou had anything to do with her brother's death. She grew up believing it was simply a terrible accident." He paused. "But one day, Kosta got drunk. And he told her that the person she had spent years resenting was Papou—the father of her daughter. He let her believe that he was responsible."

Evanthia's face turned pale. Her hands began to tremble, and Daphne reached across the table, holding them gently to steady her.

"So your mother sent Papou away," Daphne said quietly, her voice breaking, "because she believed Kosta. She thought that the man she loved—the father of her child— had killed a boy. That he had killed her own brother."

"Grandma couldn't forgive him," Yannis added, his voice heavy. "She didn't trust him anymore. She didn't want him anywhere near her daughter—near you. She told him to leave and never come back."

Evanthia's eyes widened, her breath trembling. "No. No, she wouldn't—she couldn't—"

"She did," Yannis said gently. "Kosta told us everything."

"Kosta was a drunk! Why would you believe him?" shouted Evanthia.

"He's a very old man, Mom," Yannis said gently. "At this point in his life, what reason would he have to lie?"

Evanthia shook her head, her voice cracking. "All my life… all my life I thought he abandoned us. I thought he chose someone else. I hated him for it."

Her hands trembled. "And all this time… it was her?"

Daphne's heart ached. "She was grieving. She was angry. She believed something that wasn't true."

Evanthia pressed her palms to her eyes. "I spent my whole life being angry at him, when I should have been angry at her. But how can I be angry at her now? She's gone. She's gone, and I can't ask her why. I can't ask her anything."

Yannis squeezed her hand. "You don't have to be angry at her."

Evanthia lowered her hands, her eyes shining with tears. "Then who do I get to be angry at? Who do I blame? Who do I hold responsible for all of this?"

Silence settled over the room.

Daphne swallowed hard. "If anyone is responsible for all of this, it's Kosta. I'm angry at him too. I'm trying not to be, but it's hard—so many lies for so long."

She paused for a long moment, then continued, her voice tightening. "Do you realize what this means for me? Papou wasn't my real grandfather. Kosta is."

Evanthia stared at her. "What do you mean? How can he be your grandfather?"

Yannis stepped in. "There's more, mom. Papou didn't leave for America because he'd fallen in love with another woman. I mean—he cared about her, but that wasn't why he left. Maybe he fell in love later; I don't know. None of us can know that. But that woman, Elpida, was Kosta's wife."

"What?" Evanthia cried, startled. "What on earth are you saying?"

"Kosta was violent," Yannis said, his jaw tight—"especially when he drank. And he drank a lot. He hurt Elpida. She was afraid for her life and for her daughter's. She grew close to Papou and confided in him. So when your mother sent him away—told him to go as far as possible and never come back—Elpida suggested they leave for America together. She wanted him to take her and her daughter away from Kosta."

Evanthia lifted a hand toward Yannis, as if to stop him—needing a moment to take it all in. When she finally spoke, it was with visible effort.

"And he just left?" Evanthia cried. "Without even trying to explain?"

"He tried, but she didn't believe him," Yannis said. "She probably thought he was lying because he didn't want to lose her."

"He should have tried harder—for me, for his family!" Evanthia said, tears spilling down her cheeks.

After a few moments of silence, she went on, her voice unsteady. "And… the little girl—Elpida's daughter—was she… Maria?"

"Yes," Daphne said. "Maria—my mother—was Kosta's daughter. Which makes me his granddaughter."

They sat in silence for several minutes, no one daring to speak, no one quite knowing what to say.

At last, Daphne broke the quiet. "The man we met today is evil. He caused the accident. He let your father take the blame. He let the feud destroy everything. He let your mother believe a lie. He hurt Elpida. He hurt Maria. He hurt all of us."

Evanthia's jaw tightened. "I want to see him."

Yannis shook his head gently. "Mom, what would that accomplish?"

"I need to," Evanthia insisted. "I need to look him in the eye. I need to hear him say it."

"Not like this," Daphne said softly. "Not while you're angry. Not while everything is still raw."

Evanthia stood abruptly, pacing the small kitchen. "I feel betrayed. I don't even know by whom. My mother? My father? Kosta? All of them? None of them? I don't know what to feel."

Finally Evanthia stopped pacing. She looked at Yannis, then at Daphne. Her voice softened, trembling. "You're right... I need time."

Daphne nodded. "We all do."

Yannis looked at his mom with compassion. "Give yourself a few days. Let the truth settle before you face him. And when you're ready, we'll come with you."

"Yes," added Daphne. "You won't face him alone."

The three of them sat together in the quiet kitchen, the weight of generations settling around them. Outside, the cicadas hummed in the afternoon heat, and the sea glimmered in the distance, unchanged by the truths that had shaken their world. Daphne felt the three of them connected not just by blood or history, but by the courage it took to face the past. And she knew this was not the end. It was the beginning of healing.

CHAPTER 31

Evanthia didn't come out of her room for a long time the next morning. Daphne heard her moving around—slow footsteps, the soft opening and closing of drawers, the faint clink of a cup being set on a table—but she didn't emerge. The house felt unusually quiet, as if it too were waiting for someone to speak first.

When Evanthia finally stepped into the kitchen, the light caught her face in a way that made Daphne's heart ache. She looked older somehow—not in years, but in weight. As though the truth had settled on her shoulders overnight and she was still learning how to carry it.

She sat at the table with a cup of coffee she hadn't touched. Her fingers curled around it, not for warmth, but for something to hold onto.

Daphne approached slowly. "How are you feeling?"

Evanthia let out a breath that was almost a laugh, but not quite. "Like someone took my life apart and handed it back to me in pieces."

Daphne sat across from her. "I'm sorry."

"You didn't do anything wrong," Evanthia said gently. "You didn't break anything. You just… uncovered it."

She stared at the coffee for a long moment before speaking again.

"I keep thinking about my mother," she said. "About all the stories she told me. All the things she left out. All the things she changed."

Daphne listened quietly.

"She told me my father left because he fell in love with another woman," Evanthia said. "She told me he abandoned us. She told me he chose someone else over his own family."

Her voice trembled.

"And I believed her. I believed her for decades. I hated him for it. I blamed him for everything."

Daphne reached out, but Evanthia shook her head gently, needing to finish.

"But now I know the truth. He didn't leave because he wanted to. He left because she sent him away. Because she believed something that wasn't true. Because she couldn't forgive him for something he didn't even do."

Her eyes filled with tears. After a long silence, she spoke again, her voice softer.

"I've also been thinking about Maria."

Daphne blinked. "My mother?"

"Yes. How will she react when she learns the truth? That the man she loved as her father wasn't her father at all?"

Daphne's stomach tightened. "I don't know. I honestly don't know how to tell her. I don't even know if I should tell her. She would be devastated. And I don't know if there's a reason for her to know. She's lived her whole life believing one story. I don't know if I should take that away from her."

Evanthia looked up, her eyes steady despite the exhaustion. "Family is reason enough. She should know she has family here. Real family. Not just in blood, but in love."

Daphne swallowed. "I know. But she's been through so much already. Losing her mother a few years ago, now losing Papou… she's still grieving."

Evanthia reached across the table and took Daphne's hand. "Grief doesn't erase truth. And truth doesn't erase love. We are connected. We both loved the same man as our father. That matters more than blood."

Daphne felt her throat tighten. "I never thought of it that way."

Evanthia gave a small, sad smile. "I would like to meet her. Even if she's not my sister, she's still… mine. In some way. We grew up under the same shadow. We were shaped by the same man. That makes us family."

Daphne nodded slowly. "I'll tell her. But I want to do it in person. When I go back."

"That's wise," Evanthia said. "She deserves to hear it from you, not over the phone."

Daphne rubbed her palms together, nervous. "She doesn't know anything about this. She doesn't even know that Papou still had family in Lefkada. She thinks I came here to practice my Greek, to see the island, to connect with my roots. She has no idea what I've found."

Evanthia leaned back in her chair, her expression softening. "Maybe she should come to Greece too. Maybe she should meet Kosta."

Daphne stiffened. "I don't know if she would want to. He… he wanted to hurt her when she was little. He hurt her mother."

"Yes," Evanthia said gently. "But she should have the choice. It should be her decision, not ours."

Daphne looked down at her hands. "You're right."

The room fell quiet. The morning light spilled across the table in soft gold. Daphne watched the dust motes drifting in the air, feeling strangely suspended between past and future.

Evanthia spent the next two days in a kind of quiet suspension. She moved through the house as if learning its shape again, pausing in doorways, touching the backs of chairs, staring out windows as though the landscape might offer answers her memory could not. Daphne watched her with a mixture of worry and admiration. There was a steadiness in Evanthia, even in grief — a way she held herself upright, even when the truth pressed down on her like a stone.

On the morning of the third day, Evanthia came into the kitchen with her hair pulled back and her shoulders squared. She looked rested, though her eyes still carried the faint shadows of sleepless nights.

"I'm ready," she said.

Daphne set down her cup. "To talk?"

"To see him," Evanthia said. "To see Kosta."

Yannis, who had been standing by the window, turned. "Are you sure?"

"No," Evanthia said honestly. "But I need to do it anyway."

Daphne nodded. "We'll go with you."

Evanthia gave a small, grateful smile. "I know."

The drive back to the old village felt different this time. The air was cooler, the road quiet—as if the island itself sensed the weight of what was coming. Evanthia sat in the passenger seat, rigid and silent. Yannis drove with his hands steady on the wheel, eyes fixed on the road. In the back seat, Daphne watched them both, close enough to offer support but unsure where to begin.

Yannis pulled over at exactly the same spot as when they came here with Nikolas. The three of them walked in silence. When they reached the clearing, Kosta was in the same wooden chair, facing the valley. The morning light caught the silver in his hair, making him look both ancient and strangely fragile. He didn't turn when he heard them approach, but Daphne saw his shoulders stiffen.

Evanthia stepped forward before either Daphne or Yannis could speak.

"Kosta," she said.

The old man turned slowly. His eyes landed on her, and something flickered there — recognition, regret, maybe even fear.

"You came," he said quietly.

She didn't say a word. Kosta pointed to one of the stools, but she didn't sit. She stood in front of him, her posture straight, her hands clasped in front of her. Daphne could see the tension in her shoulders, the way she held herself together with sheer will.

"I need to ask you something," Evanthia said.

Kosta nodded. "Ask."

"Why?" Her voice trembled, but she didn't look away. "Why did you let him take the blame? Why did you let my father lose everything? Why did you let my mother believe a lie that destroyed our family?"

Kosta closed his eyes. "Because I was a coward."

Evanthia's breath caught.

"I was young," Kosta continued. "And stupid. And terrified. I didn't mean to hurt the boy. It was an accident. But when it happened, I panicked. I ran. And your father… he stepped forward. He said it was him. He said he could bear it."

Evanthia's voice sharpened. "And you let him."

"Yes," Kosta whispered. "I let him."

Evanthia shook her head slowly. "Do you know what that did to us? Do you know what it did to me? I grew up believing my father abandoned me. I grew up thinking he chose another woman over his own family. I hated him for it. I hated him for decades."

Kosta's eyes glistened. "I know."

"No," Evanthia said, her voice rising. "You don't know. You don't know what it's like to spend your whole life angry at someone who didn't deserve it. You don't know what it's like to realize that the person you trusted most — my mother — lied to me. Lied to me every day of my life."

Kosta bowed his head. "I'm sorry."

Evanthia let out a shaky breath. "Sorry? You're sorry? Sorry doesn't fix anything."

"No," Kosta said. "It doesn't."

She took a step closer. "You hurt Elpida. You hurt Maria. You hurt my father. You hurt all of us. You caused so much pain!"

Kosta didn't defend himself. He didn't argue. He simply nodded, as though each accusation was a blow he knew he deserved.

"I know," he said. "And I have lived with that every day. I have lived with the knowledge that I ruined the lives of the people I loved most. I have lived with the knowledge that your father suffered because of me. That your mother suffered because of me. That Elpida suffered. That Maria suffered. That you suffered."

Evanthia's voice softened, but only slightly. "Why didn't you ever tell the truth?"

Kosta looked up at her, his eyes hollow. "Because I didn't know how. Because I was ashamed. Because I thought it was too late. Because I thought the truth would only cause more pain."

For a long moment, the clearing was silent. The wind rustled through the olive trees, carrying the scent of earth and salt. Daphne felt her heart pounding, but she stayed still, letting Evanthia lead.

Finally, Kosta spoke again, his voice barely a whisper. "You have every right to feel angry."

Evanthia looked out toward the valley. "Angry doesn't even begin to describe it." She took a deep breath. "But I needed to see you. I needed to hear you say it. I needed to know the truth from your mouth."

Kosta's eyes filled with tears. "Thank you for coming."

Evanthia shook her head. "Don't thank me. I didn't come for you. I came for myself."

Kosta nodded. "I understand."

Evanthia stepped back, her posture still straight, but her expression softer now — not forgiving, not accepting, but no longer burning with the same raw anger.

"I don't know if I'll ever forgive you," she said. "I don't know if I can."

Kosta nodded. "I don't expect you to."

"But I needed to see you," Evanthia said. "And now I have." She turned to Daphne and Yannis. "Let's go."

Daphne hesitated, glancing at Kosta. The old man looked smaller somehow, as though the truth had taken something from him too. But she followed Evanthia, knowing this moment wasn't hers to fix. As they walked back down the path, Evanthia didn't speak. She walked with her head high, her steps steady, but Daphne could feel the storm still swirling inside her. When they reached the edge of the trees, Evanthia finally stopped.

"I don't know what comes next," she said quietly.

Daphne stepped closer. "You were very brave."

Evanthia let out a breath that trembled at the edges. "I don't feel brave."

"You are," Daphne said. "You faced the truth. That's more than most people ever do."

Evanthia looked at her, her eyes softening. "Thank you."

They walked the rest of the way in silence, the island stretching out before them — ancient, patient, holding their stories the way it had held generations before them. And though nothing was resolved, something had shifted. The truth had been spoken. The past had been faced. And the path forward, though uncertain, no longer felt impossible.

CHAPTER 32

Daphne spent her last morning in Lefkada packing slowly, almost ritualistically, as if each folded shirt and tucked-away item marked the closing of a chapter she wasn't entirely ready to end. The small guest room felt different now — not just because she had lived in it for days, but because she had changed inside it. She had arrived with a suitcase full of questions and a heart full of longing. She was leaving with answers she hadn't expected, truths she hadn't imagined, and a family she hadn't known she had.

She paused with her hands resting on the small pouch that had held the mechanism's cylindrical weight. The fabric was soft from handling, the edges slightly frayed. The weight was still in the mechanism in the basement. Daphne decided to leave it there. It was exactly where it belonged. She didn't have any use for it in Astoria anyway. Its destination was here, its home was here, in the mechanism. And its purpose had been fulfilled. The mechanism had revealed what it needed to reveal. She remembered her grandfather's words in the note she and Yannis had found inside it.

Follow the path with courage.

She had. And the path had led her somewhere she never could have predicted — into the heart of a story that had been waiting for her long before she was born.

She slipped the empty pouch into her bag and zipped it closed, her breath catching for a moment. Leaving felt wrong and right at the same time — like stepping away from something precious but stepping toward something necessary.

When she stepped outside, the morning sun wrapped her in warmth. The air smelled of pine, sea salt, and the faint sweetness of blooming basil. Evanthia and Yannis stood near the gate, waiting for her. Their expressions were composed, but Daphne could see the tightness around their eyes, the way their hands fidgeted slightly, betraying the emotions they were trying to hold steady.

"You're really leaving today," Evanthia said, her voice gentle but strained.

Daphne nodded. "My flight is tonight. And it's a long drive from here."

Evanthia stepped closer, her eyes searching Daphne's face. "I wish you could stay longer."

"I know," Daphne said softly. "I wish I could too."

There was a pause — not awkward, but full. Full of everything they had learned, everything they had shared, everything they had survived together in such a short time. The silence felt like a blanket around them, warm and heavy.

Evanthia exhaled slowly. "These days… they changed me. They changed everything I thought I knew."

"Me too," Daphne said. "More than I can explain."

Yannis nodded, his expression tender. "You came here looking for your grandfather. And you found… us."

Daphne smiled, though her eyes stung. "I did."

Evanthia reached out and took her hands, her grip warm and steady. "You're family, Daphne. Not because of blood. Because of everything we've walked through together. Because of the truth we faced. Because of the love we share for the same people."

Daphne swallowed hard. "I feel the same. I really do."

"Come on, we're not saying goodbye yet," said Yannis trying to look composed. "You two get in the car. You don't want to miss your bus, Daphne—although we'd love it if you did. Then you could stay a little longer."

Evanthia ignored him. "Promise me you'll come back," she said, squeezing Daphne's hands.

"I will," Daphne said. "And next time… I'll try to bring my mother. I want her to meet you. I want her to see this place. To understand where she comes from. Where *we* come from."

Evanthia's eyes softened, filling with something like hope. "I would love that. Even if we're not sisters… she's still my family. And I'd like to know her."

Daphne nodded. "I'll tell her everything when I get back. All of it."

"All right, get in the car," Yannis said again. "Now, please. We'll be late."

On the way to the bus station, all three of them were quiet. Only when they were almost there did Evanthia speak. "You're not leaving us," she said quietly. "You're just going home for a little while."

Daphne felt her throat tighten. "I'll be back within the year. I promise."

Evanthia smiled through her tears. "Good. Because we're not done with you yet."

They all laughed softly, the sound warm and fragile. It felt like a moment suspended in time — a moment she knew she would replay in her mind long after she returned to Astoria.

When the bus arrived, Evanthia and Yannis hugged her one last time. Evanthia held her tightly, as though trying to memorize the shape of her, the warmth of her, the reality of her presence.

"Tell Maria everything," she whispered. "Tell her she has a home here. And that she has family waiting for her."

"I will," Daphne said.

"And come back soon," Yannis added. "Don't make us wait too long."

"I won't," Daphne promised.

The driver called for final boarding.

Daphne took a slow breath, squeezed their hands one last time, and climbed onto the bus.

"Text us when you get there. And when you get to the airport. And when you land," Evanthia called out.

"I will," Daphne promised.

She chose a window seat halfway down the aisle. As the bus pulled away, she pressed her forehead to the glass, watching Evanthia and Yannis shrink into the distance — two figures standing side by side, waving until the road curved and they disappeared from view.

The island rolled past her in fragments — olive groves shimmering in the sun, stone houses with terracotta roofs, glimpses of the sea flashing between the trees. The bus hummed steadily along the winding roads, carrying her away from Lefkada and toward Athens.

But her heart felt tethered to the island, as if part of her had stayed behind. She had come to Lefkada searching for her grandfather. She was leaving with a family. And she knew — with a certainty that surprised her — that she would return. Soon.

The ride to Athens took several hours. Daphne dozed for a while, waking to the soft murmur of other passengers and the rhythmic thrum of the tires on the road. When the bus finally pulled into the Athens station, the city greeted her with its familiar chaos — honking cars, hurried footsteps, the scent of roasted chestnuts drifting from a nearby vendor. She stepped off the bus, stretching her legs, feeling the weight of the journey settle into her bones.

Her phone buzzed.

A message from Evanthia.

Did you arrive safely?

Daphne smiled and typed back.

Just got off the bus.

A moment later:

Good. Let us know when you get to the airport.

Daphne pressed the phone to her chest, feeling loved.

Late in the evening, as Daphne waited to board the plane, she was pleasantly surprised by how much of the Greek around her she could understand. Bits of conversation floated past—casual jokes, quiet complaints, a mother soothing a tired child—and this time the words didn't slip away from her. The fact that she was catching so much encouraged her. She was determined to keep up with her Greek lessons and become fluent. She was Greek-

American, but in that moment the Greek part of her felt stronger than ever.

She found an empty seat near the gate and sat down. Then she pulled out her phone. There was one more goodbye she needed to make — one that felt lighter, but no less important.

She dialed Tasos.

He answered on the second ring. "Daphne?"

His voice was warm, surprised, and something in her chest loosened at the sound of it. She hadn't realized how much she had come to associate his voice with comfort, with steadiness, with the strange sense of belonging she had found here.

"Hi," she said. "I just wanted to call before I leave. To thank you again. For everything."

"You don't have to thank me," he said. "I'm glad I could help."

"You helped more than you know," Daphne said. "And I wanted you to know that I'll be back. Which means… I want to continue our lessons."

There was a pause — a soft, hopeful pause that made her smile.

"I would like that," Tasos said. "Very much."

Daphne smiled. "Good."

"But…" he added, clearing his throat, "I was thinking… maybe I could have some lessons too. English lessons."

"English lessons?" Daphne asked, amused. "Your English is perfect."

Tasos laughed. "Yes, sure, I know grammar and vocabulary. But my accent is terrible. I know it is. If you say anything to the contrary, I know it's because you're trying to be nice."

"It's not terrible," Daphne said, laughing. "I've never had any trouble understanding you."

"Yeah right," he insisted, "I speak like a Greek fisherman who swallowed a dictionary."

Daphne laughed harder. "Your accent is really not that bad."

"It is," he said. "I want to speak good, understandable English. Because…" He hesitated, then continued, "because I would love to visit New York sometime soon."

Daphne's breath caught — not in shock, but in a warm, unexpected flutter. The idea of Tasos in New York — walking through Astoria, meeting her mother, seeing her world — felt strangely right.

"I would really like that," she said softly.

The moment the words left her mouth — *"I'd really like it if you visited New York"* — Daphne felt a warm flutter in her chest. It was excitement, yes, but also something else.

Something sharper. A tiny, ridiculous panic that crept in through the back door of her mind.

Because if Tasos came to New York… If he spent time with her every day… If he saw her in her real, unfiltered life…

Would he notice? Would he realize she was still, in some small stubborn corner of her mind, a hypochondriac? The thought made her stomach tighten. She had worked so hard to get better — years of reading, journaling, breathing exercises, late-night videos about anxiety and negative thoughts. She had made real progress. She *knew* she had. She wasn't the girl who used to search every symptom online or check her pulse ten times a day. But still… the old habits lingered like shadows.

She took a slow breath, reminding herself how far she had come. She had traveled alone. She had touched a disgusting fence and survived. She had slept in a guesthouse and only disinfected everything once. She had stayed in the spare room at Evanthia's house without disinfecting the door handle or the light switch. She had done things she never would have dared a few years ago.

Maybe — just maybe — she could do even more. Maybe she could do a little self-therapy again. Revisit the books she had underlined. Rewatch the videos that had once calmed her. Maybe she could even try something new — hypnotherapy, or whatever people were doing these days to quiet the anxious parts of their brains.

The idea steadied her. She had time. Tasos wasn't coming tomorrow. She didn't need to be perfect — she just needed to keep growing, the way she already had.

The panic softened. The warmth returned. Her shoulders loosened. She had barely heard what Tasos had said, her thoughts having taken over her mind. Three breaths steadied her, and she tuned back in just in time to catch his next words.

"Then I will practice," Tasos said. "So when I come, you will not pretend you don't know me."

"I would never pretend that," Daphne said.

There was a smile in his voice when he replied. "Good."

Daphne allowed herself to imagine it — Tasos in New York, walking beside her, seeing her life, meeting her mother, laughing with her in the city she called home.

She smiled. She had time. And she would be ready.

They said goodbye, and Daphne slipped her phone back into her bag, her heart lighter than it had been in days. The future felt uncertain, but in a way that excited her — like a story still being written.

The flight home was long and quiet. Daphne sat by the window, staring out at the endless stretch of clouds, her thoughts looping in slow, heavy circles.

She replayed the goodbyes. She replayed the truths. She replayed the moment she would soon have to face. Telling her mother. Her stomach twisted at the thought. She imagined Maria's face — the softness around her eyes, the way she always tucked her hair behind her ear when she was nervous, the way she smiled when she talked about Papou.

She imagined that smile faltering. Breaking.

How do you tell someone their entire story is different than they believed?

Daphne didn't know. But she knew she had to try.

When the plane landed in New York, the familiar rush of noise and movement hit her all at once — the chatter of passengers, the rolling of suitcases, the distant echo of announcements over the loudspeakers. It felt jarring after the quiet of the island, like stepping from a dream into a world that had kept moving without her.

Outside, the air was colder, sharper. She pulled her jacket tighter around her and breathed in the scent of the city — exhaust, roasted nuts from a nearby cart. She took a taxi home, watching the skyline rise in the distance. The buildings looked impossibly tall after the low stone houses of Lefkada. The streets buzzed with life, horns blaring, people weaving through crosswalks with practiced urgency. But inside the cab, Daphne felt strangely still. As if she were carrying a piece of the island with her.

When she reached her apartment, she dropped her suitcase by the door and sank onto the couch. The room felt familiar but distant, like a place she had once lived but no longer belonged to entirely. She stared at the ceiling for a long moment, letting the quiet settle around her.

She pulled out her phone and sent a message to Yannis.

Good evening, Lefkada. I made it safely.

A few seconds later, her phone buzzed.

Good evening, New York.

It's still morning over here. Seven hours behind, remember?

Oh, right! Did you have a good trip?

Yes, but I'm exhausted.

Get some rest. We miss you.

Me too. Kisses to Evanthia.

Daphne took a shower and went straight to bed for a short nap. When she woke up, she realized she couldn't wait until the next day to go to her mother's. She needed to go today. The truth sat on her chest like a weight she had to set down. She got dressed, grabbed her coat, and headed out. The walk to her mother's apartment felt longer than usual, each step heavy with what she was about to do.

When she reached the building, she paused at the door, taking a slow breath. She could hear her heartbeat in her ears, steady but fast.

She knocked. A moment later, the door opened.

Maria stood there, her face lighting up with joy. "Daphne! Finally!"

Daphne smiled, though her chest tightened. "Hi, mom."

They held each other for a long time—Maria not wanting to let go because she had missed her daughter, and Daphne clinging to her as if bracing herself for the painful truth she was about to lay on her mother.

CHAPTER 33

Maria led Daphne into the living room, still smiling, still unaware of the weight her daughter carried. The apartment smelled like thyme and lemon — the scent of home, of childhood, of safety. A pot simmered on the stove, and the soft hum of the heater filled the quiet spaces between them.

"Sit, *koukla mou*," Maria said, brushing Daphne's arm affectionately. "You must be exhausted. Tell me everything. Did you see the beaches? Did you go to Porto Katsiki? Did you practice your Greek? Did you—"

"Mom," Daphne said firmly.

Maria stopped. Her smile faded, replaced by a crease of concern between her brows.

"What is it?" she asked softly. "Did something happen?"

Daphne sat on the couch, her hands clasped tightly in her lap. Maria sat beside her, turning her body fully toward her daughter, waiting.

Daphne took a slow breath.

"I didn't go to Lefkada for tourism," she said. "Not really."

Maria blinked. "What do you mean?"

"I went because of Papou," Daphne said. "Because of the letter he left me."

Maria's face softened with recognition. "Ah. The letter. Are you finally ready to tell me what was in it?"

Daphne swallowed. "Mom… I found something. I found people."

Maria's expression shifted — confusion, then curiosity, then something like fear. "People?"

"Family," Daphne said quietly. "Your family."

Maria froze.

"My… what?"

"Your father's family," Daphne said.

Maria stared at her, her breath caught somewhere between disbelief and dread. "Daphne… my father didn't have family in Lefkada. He didn't have siblings, and his parents died long before he left. As far as I know, he didn't have anyone else."

"That's not true," Daphne whispered. "He left family behind—some of it is still there. And I met them."

Maria's face went pale.

"Mom… Papou didn't leave because he wanted to. He left because of something that happened when he was young. Something he took the blame for. Something that wasn't his fault."

"What are you talking about?" Maria asked, puzzled.

"There was an accident," Daphne said. "A little boy died. And Papou was blamed. But he didn't do it. His brother did."

Maria's breath hitched. "His… brother?"

"Yes," Daphne said. "Kosta."

Maria stared at her, stunned. "My father had a brother?"

"Yes," Daphne said. "And he's still alive."

Maria covered her mouth with her hand, tears spilling over. "I don't… I don't understand. Why didn't he tell me? Why didn't he ever say anything?"

"Because he was protecting his brother," Daphne said. She hesitated for a few seconds, then continued. "There was a woman—not your mother—a woman named Alexandra. She loved Papou and he loved her. They had a daughter, Evanthia."

"Wait. Please, wait. My father was with another woman before my mother? And…are you telling me that I have a half-sister?"

Daphne took a deep breath. "You have family. Evanthia's mom sent Papou away because someone lied to her that he was responsible for her brother's death. Her brother was the little boy."

Maria was unable to speak. Daphne continued. "So Evanthia's mom, Alexandra, couldn't forgive him. She told him to leave and never come back."

Maria shook her head violently. "No. No, that can't be true."

"It is, Mom," Daphne said softly.

"And my mom? When did he meet her? How…"

Daphne interrupted her. "I'll tell you about your mom, but promise me to be strong for what you're about to hear. And I need you to keep in mind that Papou hid the truth from you to protect you, because he didn't want to hurt you, because he thought the truth would destroy everything."

Maria nodded, and Daphne continued. She spoke about Perigiali, about Agios Nikitas, about the old house. Then she gathered all the strength she had and finally spoke about Kosta, about the drinking and the violence. She talked about how brave Papou was, to take Maria and her mother away from the man who was harming them, to save Maria from her own father.

Maria leaned forward, pressing her forehead to Daphne's shoulder. Daphne wrapped her arms around her, holding her tightly as her mother cried — deep, aching sobs that seemed to come from a place she had never touched before.

After a while, Maria pulled back and wiped her tears. "Tell me about Evanthia," she said. Daphne told her about Evanthia — the woman who, like Maria, had grown up believing a lie. About Yannis — the nephew Maria never knew she had. About Nikolas — Papou's best friend.

Maria listened without interrupting, her face shifting through disbelief, grief, anger, sorrow, and something else — something like recognition.

When Daphne finished, Maria sat very still.

"So… Evanthia," she said quietly. "She's not my sister."

"No," Daphne said. "She's your cousin."

Maria nodded slowly. "But she loved him. She loved my father. Just like I did."

"Yes," Daphne said. "She did."

Maria closed her eyes. "And Kosta… he hurt my mother."

"Yes."

"And he wanted to hurt me."

"Yes."

Maria opened her eyes again, and they were filled with something fierce and fragile all at once.

"I don't know if I can forgive him," she said. "I don't know if I want to."

"You don't have to," Daphne said gently. "But I wanted you to have the choice."

Maria nodded. "I would like to meet them," she whispered. "Evanthia. Yannis."

Daphne felt her chest loosen. "They want to meet you too."

Maria took a shaky breath. "Maybe we could go to Greece together."

"Of course," Daphne said. "Whenever you're ready."

Maria reached for her daughter's hand, squeezing it tightly.

"Let's go soon."

They sat together in the quiet living room, the weight of the past settling around them — heavy, yes, but no longer unbearable. The truth had broken something open, but it had also made space for something new. Healing. Connection. Family.

CHAPTER 34

Maria insisted on cooking dinner. It wasn't simply hospitality — it was her way of grounding herself, of reclaiming a sense of rhythm after the emotional earthquake of the last few days. Cooking had always been her anchor. When life felt uncertain, she chopped onions, squeezed lemons, seasoned chicken with oregano and olive oil. She moved through the kitchen with a kind of quiet determination, as though each familiar motion stitched her back together.

When Daphne arrived at her mother's house, the sky outside was streaked with lavender and rose, the last light of evening settling gently over the city. The hallway smelled faintly of roasted chicken, garlic, and lemon — scents that wrapped around Daphne like a memory. She paused for a moment before knocking, letting the warmth of the smell settle into her chest.

Maria opened the door with a soft smile. *"Kalosorises, koukla mou.* Come in. Dinner is almost ready."

Daphne stepped inside, slipping off her coat. The living room lights were dimmed, casting a soft glow across the framed photographs on the walls. The kitchen was warm, the oven humming, the table already set with plates and glasses.

Maria moved around the kitchen with practiced ease, stirring a pot, checking the oven, wiping her hands on a towel. She was quieter than usual, but there was a steadiness in her movements that hadn't been there the day before. Something had settled inside her — not peace, not yet, but a kind of clarity.

"Sit," Maria said, gesturing to the table. "I want to talk to you before we eat."

Daphne sat, her heart tightening slightly. "Of course."

Maria took a deep breath, then joined her at the table, folding her hands in front of her. Her eyes were clear, focused, and full of something that looked like resolve.

"I've made a decision," she said.

Daphne straightened. "About what?"

"About Greece," Maria said. "About Lefkada. About… everything."

Daphne held her breath.

"I am ready to go. I don't want to wait," Maria said softly.

Daphne felt her chest loosen, warmth blooming behind her ribs. "Mom… really?"

"Yes," Maria said. "How about next month?"

Daphne reached across the table and squeezed her mother's hand. "Yes! Let's do it. I'm so glad."

Maria smiled, though her eyes glistened. "I think your grandfather would want that."

They sat in silence for a moment, letting the decision settle between them like a soft, steady light. It felt like the beginning of something — not closure, but movement. A door opening rather than closing.

Then Maria cleared her throat.

"There's something else I forgot to tell you," she said. "Something that happened while you were gone."

Daphne frowned. "What is it?"

Maria looked almost sheepish. "I went to your apartment a couple of days ago."

"You did?"

"Yes," Maria said. "I wanted to make sure everything was okay. No leaks, no burglars, no... I don't know. I just wanted to check."

Daphne smiled. "That's sweet."

"Well," Maria continued, "I also listened to your answering machine. Just in case there was something urgent."

Daphne blinked. "My answering machine?"

"Yes," Maria said. "And there was a message. From the Astoria Historical Society."

Daphne felt a jolt of surprise. "Really? What did they say?"

"They didn't say much," Maria said. "Just that they wanted you to call them back as soon as possible."

Daphne reached for her phone. "I'll call them now. They should still be there—it's twenty to five."

Maria nodded and stood to check the oven while Daphne dialed the number.

The archivist answered on the second ring.

"Hello, Astoria Historical Society, this is Martha."

"Hi, Martha," Daphne said. "This is Daphne Stavrides, Yannis Papadakis's granddaughter. I think you left me a message?"

"Oh! Yes, Daphne. Thank you for calling back."

Her voice brightened with recognition.

"I wanted to let you know," she continued, "that our former director stopped by a few days ago. I asked him about the letter he had sent to your grandpa and the model he had asked about."

Daphne's pulse quickened. "And?"

"Well," Martha said, "he told me that your grandfather brought it in himself. Personally."

Daphne blinked. "He did?"

"Yes," Martha said. "I didn't know that at the time because I was out sick for a couple of weeks when he dropped it off. But the director remembered it clearly. He said that Mr. Papadakis was very particular about how it should be stored."

Daphne felt her breath catch. "Stored? Where?"

"In our storage area," Martha said. "It's been in there for a while. The director asked me to bring it out because we're preparing a new exhibit on historical scientific instruments."

Daphne's mind raced. "What does it look like?"

"Well," Martha said, sounding almost amused, "it's an exact replica of the Antikythera mechanism."

Daphne froze.

The Antikythera mechanism. The ancient Greek astronomical calculator. The most mysterious artifact of antiquity. Her grandfather had built a replica.

But—

It had nothing to do with Lefkada. Nothing to do with the letter. Nothing to do with the mechanism she found on the island. It was a separate project entirely. A different secret. A different story.

"I see," Daphne said quietly.

Martha continued, "The old director said he'd love to keep it for our upcoming exposition. It's a remarkable piece. But of course, it's yours to decide."

Daphne swallowed. "I think… I think you can keep it for the exposition. For a few months."

"That would be wonderful," Martha said. "And after that?"

Daphne hesitated, then spoke with certainty.

"After that, I would have to think about it. Perhaps I'll send it to the Metropolitan Museum of Art in New York. I think that's where it belongs."

Martha let out a low whistle. "The Met. That's quite a home for it. I'll make a note of it," Martha said. "And thank you, Daphne. It's a beautiful piece. Truly."

They said goodbye, and Daphne hung up, staring at her phone for a long moment.

Maria returned to the table, wiping her hands on a towel. "What did they say?"

Daphne told her everything — the Historical Society, the old director, the replica, the exposition, the Met. Maria listened, her expression shifting from surprise to wonder.

"He really was something," she whispered. "Your grandfather."

Daphne nodded. "He was."

Maria reached across the table and took her daughter's hand again.

"We'll go to Greece," she said. "We'll visit his family. Our family. We'll see everything. And we'll bring him with us. In our hearts."

Daphne squeezed her hand.

"Yes," she said. "We will."

"Your dad can stay here. I think he'll survive by himself for a couple of weeks," Maria said and they both chuckled.

"I heard that. I'll be fine. Make sure to take a lot of pictures," said Daphne's dad who had just woken up from his nap.

Dinner was warm and comforting — roasted chicken, lemon potatoes, a simple salad with olive oil and oregano. They talked about practical things — flights, timing, work schedules — but beneath it all was a quiet current of something deeper. Connection. Anticipation. Family.

After dinner, Daphne helped her mother wash the dishes. They worked in silence, the kind that felt easy and full. When they finished, Maria dried her hands and turned to her daughter.

"I'm proud of you," she said softly. "For going. For finding the truth. For bringing it back to me."

Daphne felt her throat tighten. "I didn't do it alone."

"No," Maria said. "But you were brave. And you followed the path he left for you."

Daphne nodded, feeling the truth of it settle inside her.

When she left her mother's house that night, the air outside was crisp and cool. The city lights shimmered against the dark sky, and Daphne felt something she hadn't felt in a long time. A sense of direction. A sense of purpose. A sense of belonging — not just to the past, but to the future she and her mother were about to build together.

CHAPTER 35

Daphne sat at her small kitchen table long after the city had gone quiet. The lights outside her window glowed in soft halos, blurred by the thin winter fog drifting over Astoria. Her tea had gone cold. Her pen lay untouched beside a blank sheet of paper.

She had been trying to write this letter for days. Every time she picked up the pen, her hand froze. Every time she tried to form the words, her throat tightened. Forgiveness was a complicated thing — heavier than she expected, more tangled than she wanted it to be.

But she kept thinking of Kosta sitting in that wooden chair in the clearing, his hands folded over his cane, his eyes full of regret. She kept thinking of the way his voice had trembled when he spoke of her grandfather. She kept thinking of the years he had carried the truth alone.

And she kept thinking of time — how it moved whether she was ready or not.

She didn't know how long he had left. She didn't know if she would see him again before he was gone. She didn't know if she would ever truly forgive him. All she knew was that she didn't want him to die believing she hated him. She took a slow breath, picked up the pen, and began to write.

Papou Kosta,

I've been trying to find the right words, but I don't know if there are any. Maybe there never will be. Maybe the truth is that some things can't be said perfectly — they can only be said honestly.

So I'm going to try.

I've been thinking a lot about what happened. About what you told me. About the choices you made, and the ones that were made for you. I've been thinking about the weight you carried, and how long you carried it alone.

I don't know if I'm ready to forgive everything. I don't even know if I understand everything or if I ever will.

But I don't want you to leave this world thinking I hate you.

I don't.

I'm hurt. I'm confused. I'm still trying to make sense of it all. But I don't hate you. I see the pain you've lived with. I see the love you had for my grandfather. I see the regret in your eyes. And I see the part of you that tried — even if it was too late, even if it wasn't enough.

I want you to know that I'm trying too.

I'm trying to understand. I'm trying to heal. I'm trying to find a way forward that honors the truth without letting it destroy what's left.

I don't know if forgiveness is something that happens all at once. Maybe it's something that grows slowly, like a seed planted in difficult soil.

I want you to know that I'm not closing the door. I'm not turning away. I'm not giving up on the possibility of peace.

I'm writing this now because I don't want to wait until it's too late. I don't want to carry the regret of silence. And I don't want you to carry the fear that you are hated.

You're not.

I hope I can visit soon. I hope I can bring my mother with me. I hope we can sit together — not in anger, not in fear, but in something closer to understanding.

Until then, please take care of yourself.
Please know that I'm thinking of you.
And please know that I'm trying.

With hope,
Daphne

Daphne set the pen down and stared at the letter. Her chest felt tight, but not in the same way it had before. This tightness was different — not fear, not anger, but something like release.

She took a picture of the letter and emailed it to Tasos, asking him to translate it in English. Tasos sent it back within an hour. Daphne printed the translation, folded the paper carefully, and slipped it into an envelope. She didn't know if she would mail it tomorrow or next week or hand it to him in person someday. But she knew she needed to write it now, while the words were still warm. She wasn't ready to forgive him fully. But she was ready to try. And for now, that was enough.

CHAPTER 36

Daphne had been carrying a quiet ache since returning from Lefkada. An ache shaped like love and grief and all the words she never had the chance to say to her grandfather. She had written a letter to Kosta, but this one felt different. This one felt heavier, gentler, more sacred.

Papou Yannis was gone. She would never see him again. Never hear his voice. Never feel his steady presence beside her. But she could still speak to him. She could still tell him what she hadn't been able to say while he was alive. She picked up her pen and she began.

Papou,

I don't know if writing this will make anything easier. Maybe it won't. Maybe it will just make the missing you sharper. But I need to say these things, even if you'll never read them.

You were my Papou. You are my Papou. You always will be.

Not because you raised me. Not because you taught me things. Not because you welcomed me into your life with open arms.

But because you were my blood. Because I was yours. Because I was the granddaughter of your brother — and you loved me as if I were your own from the very first moment.

I felt it that love, and I still do.
I want you to know that I love you. Not because of obligation, not because of the story we uncovered, but because of who you were. Because of your gentleness. Because of your strength. Because of the way you looked at me like you had been waiting for me your whole life.

I understand why you hid the truth. I understand why you stayed silent. You were trying to protect everyone — my mother, grandma, Evanthia, Alexandra, even me.
You were trying to hold a family together with your own two hands.

I don't blame you. I don't resent you. I don't think less of you. If anything, I see you more clearly now. And I love you more for it.

I keep thinking about the letter you left for me in Greek. Do you know how many times I got frustrated with you for that? How many times I stared at those words and thought, Why couldn't he have written this in English? Why did he have to torture me like this?

You would have laughed. I know you did it on purpose. You always did enjoy watching me struggle through Greek verbs.

But I want you to know something that would make you proud: I can understand every single word now. Every curve of every letter. Every phrase. Every meaning. Your language is mine now too.

Your words are mine. Your story is mine. And I'm grateful for that — even if you did make me suffer through the lessons.

I wish I could tell you these things in person. I wish I could sit beside you one more time. I wish I could hug you again, feel your hand on my shoulder, hear you say my name in that soft, warm way you had.

I wish I could bring your daughter to you. I wish she could have seen you, even once, even for a moment. I wish she could have felt what I felt — the safety, the love, the quiet strength.

I'm going to try to visit Lefkada again soon. I'm going with mom. I want her to see the place where you grew up, the place where you loved, the place where you carried your grief and your hope.

I want her to know you the way I did — through the stories, the land, the people who loved you.

I hope you knew how much you meant to me, Papou. I hope you knew how much I loved you.

I'm sorry for the guilt you felt. There's nothing to forgive. You were brave and strong, and I hope I have even a tiny bit of that in me.

And I hope you're at peace now.
Truly at peace.

With all my love,
Daphne

Daphne put her pen down, her vision blurring with tears. She pressed the letter to her chest, holding it there for a long moment, as if the paper could bridge the distance between life and death. Then she folded it carefully and placed it in the drawer of her nightstand — a quiet place, a safe place, a place where the words could rest.

She turned off the lamp, letting the room fall into darkness. Outside, the city breathed. Inside, her heart ached — but it also felt lighter.

She whispered into the quiet:

"Goodnight, Papou."

CHAPTER 37

Daphne followed Yannis down the narrow wooden staircase, the old boards creaking softly beneath their feet. The basement smelled faintly of earth and olive wood, the same scent she remembered from the first time she had descended these steps. The air was cool, still, almost reverent — as if the walls themselves understood what was about to happen.

Above them, the muffled sounds of voices drifted down — Maria and Evanthia in the kitchen, talking over coffee. Their voices rose and fell in waves, sometimes soft, sometimes bright, sometimes trembling. At one point, Daphne heard a burst of laughter, followed by a sound that was unmistakably a sob.

She paused on the stairs, listening.

Yannis stopped too, turning slightly toward her.

"They're doing well," he said quietly.

Daphne nodded. "They are."

Another ripple of laughter floated down, warm and fragile.

"Probably crying and laughing at the same time," she murmured.

Yannis smiled. "That's how healing sounds."

They continued downward, step by slow step, until they reached the bottom. The basement was dim, lit only by a single hanging bulb that cast a soft circle of light over the old workbench. Dust motes drifted lazily in the air. The mechanism sat exactly where they had left it — ancient, mysterious, waiting.

Daphne approached it with a kind of reverence. Her heart beat steadily, but her hands trembled.

Yannis stood beside her, his presence steady and grounding.

She turned to him. "Do you have yours?"

He nodded. "Yes. I finished it last night." He reached into the pocket of his shirt and pulled out a folded piece of paper. He looked at it for a moment, his eyes softening.

Daphne reached into her own pocket and pulled out her letter — the one she had written to Papou Yannis in New York, the one she had folded and unfolded a dozen times, the one she had slept beside for nights because she couldn't bear to put it anywhere else. She placed it next to his.

For a moment, neither of them spoke. The basement felt like a sanctuary — a place where grief and love could sit side by side without contradiction.

Yannis cleared his throat softly. "Are you ready?"

Daphne nodded, though she wasn't sure anyone could ever be ready for something like this.

They each picked up their letters. Daphne folded hers again — once, twice, three times — until it was small enough to fit into the narrow slit of the mechanism. Yannis did the same, his hands steady but his breath uneven.

Together, they slid their letters into the opening where they had once found Papou's note — the place where truth had first revealed itself, where everything had begun.

The paper disappeared into the darkness inside the mechanism.

Daphne placed her hand on the side of the device. "Turn it," she whispered.

Yannis nodded.

He grasped the handle and began to turn. The gears shifted with a soft metallic whisper, the sound familiar and ancient, like the turning of time itself. Daphne watched the wheels rotate, watched the shadows move across the brass, watched the mechanism swallow their words into its hidden chambers.

When the final gear clicked into place, Yannis stepped back.

Daphne reached forward and removed the cylinder — the same one that had once revealed her grandfather's message. It was cool in her hands, heavier than she remembered, as if it carried not just metal but memory. She held it to her chest. Yannis looked at her, his eyes shining. Then, without warning, he stepped forward and pulled her into a tight hug. Daphne stiffened for a moment, caught off guard, and then hugged him back. She rested her cheek against his shoulder, holding on as his body trembled. That was when she realized he was crying. Her own tears came fast, unstoppable.

They stood like that for a long time — two people bound by blood, by loss, by love, by the strange and beautiful truth that had brought them together.

When she finally pulled back, she wiped her cheeks and sniffed. "You're a man from Lefkada," she said, trying to smile. "You're not supposed to cry."

Yannis let out a wet laugh. "If you tell anyone, I'll deny it."

She laughed too — a soft, broken sound that felt like release.

They stood there for another moment, breathing in the quiet, letting the weight of the moment settle. Then Daphne looked toward the stairs.

"Come on," she said gently. "We've left our family waiting upstairs."

Yannis nodded, wiping his eyes with the back of his hand. "Yes. Let's go."

They climbed the stairs slowly, side by side. As they reached the top, the sound of laughter drifted toward them — bright, warm, alive. Maria and Evanthia were still at the table, leaning toward each other, hands clasped, eyes shining. Daphne paused in the doorway, watching them. Then Yannis came up beside her, and together they walked in and took their seats at the table with their mothers. Evanthia poured tea, and soon all four of them were holding warm mugs in their hands. They lifted them at the same time.

"To family," Evanthia said.

"To family," the others echoed.

Epilogue

Papou Yannis's letter to Daphne

Αγαπημένη μου Δάφνη, λατρεμένο μου εγγόνι,

Αν ήξερες πόση χαρά έφερες στη ζωή μου από τη στιγμή που σε κράτησα πρώτη φορά στην αγκαλιά μου. Το γέλιο σου, το πείσμα σου, τα φωτεινά σου μάτια… όλα μου θύμιζαν ότι η ζωή ήταν όμορφη. Ακόμα και στις σκοτεινές μου στιγμές, η ύπαρξή σου μου έδινε χαρά. Κι υπήρχαν σκοτεινές στιγμές, γεμάτες λύπη κι ενοχή. Ενοχή για όσα άφησα πίσω. Ενοχή για την αλήθεια που κράτησα κρυφή.

Γι' αυτό σου γράφω αυτό το γράμμα, όμορφό μου κορίτσι. Υπάρχει μια αλήθεια που θέλω να σου πω, μια αλήθεια που κουβαλούσα για πολλά χρόνια, που με βάραινε όλο και περισσότερο με τον καιρό. Δεν βρήκα ποτέ το θάρρος να την πω. Ήρθε η ώρα να τη μάθεις, να τη δεις από κοντά, να τη ζήσεις.

Πρέπει να πας στη Λευκάδα. Να βρεις το παλιό σπίτι στον λόφο. Στο σπίτι αυτό έχεις οικογένεια. Εκεί είναι κρυμμένος ένας θησαυρός που σε περιμένει. Για να τον ανοίξεις, θα χρειαστείς ένα κομμάτι, που θα το βρεις στο γραφείο μου, στο τρίτο συρτάρι. Χωρίς αυτό το κομμάτι, δεν μπορεί να λειτουργήσει. Να ξέρεις ότι δεν πρόκειται για χρυσάφι ούτε για χρήματα, αλλά για κάτι πολύ πιο πολύτιμο. Κάτι που θα σου δώσει δύναμη, αλλά και πόνο. Σου ζητώ συγγνώμη γι' αυτό. Όμως ο πόνος είναι μέρος του μυστικού, μέρος της ζωής, μέρος της ιστορίας.

Αυτό που θα ανακαλύψεις μπορεί να σε ταράξει. Μπορεί να σε μπερδέψει. Ίσως και να σε θυμώσει. Αλλά σου υπόσχομαι, κορίτσι μου — θα αξίζει.

Συγχώρεσέ με που έκρυψα την αλήθεια τόσο καιρό. Συγχώρεσέ με για τη σιωπή που κράτησα, πιστεύοντας ότι προστάτευα αυτούς που αγαπούσα. Η μητέρα σου δεν γνωρίζει την αλήθεια. Αποφάσισε εσύ αν πρέπει να τη μάθει. Σου έχω εμπιστοσύνη. Πάντα είχες μια σοφή καρδιά.

Ελπίζω να μην έχεις θυμώσει που έγραψα αυτό το γράμμα στα ελληνικά, όπως θύμωνες μικρή όταν σου διάβαζα ιστορίες που δεν καταλάβαινες. Αλλά η γλώσσα μας είναι δώρο. Από τα μεγαλύτερα που μπορούσα να σου αφήσω. Και από εκεί που βρίσκομαι τώρα, ξέρω ότι μπορείς να διαβάσεις κάθε λέξη αυτού του γράμματος χωρίς βοήθεια. Και αυτό με κάνει περήφανο όσο τίποτα άλλο.

Με όλη μου την αγάπη,
Ο παππούς σου,
Γιάννης